CRIME PAYS

THE COLLECTION

ERIC REESE

ISBN: 978-1-925988-58-1

"You gotta be able to smile through the bullshit."

- TUPAC SHAKUR

CONTENTS

A book must be the axe for the frozen sea
within us.

- FRANZ KAFKA

XUAN LANG

While seeking revenge, dig two graves - one for
yourself.

- DOUGLAS HORTON

Xuan Lang pulled his suitcase across the white tiles, staring at Airport Exit B. There were people rushing inside the terminal from the rain, while Xuan only wanted a taxi to his new address. Mr. Lang had arrived in the United States for six months and wasn't sure if he'd be finished his mission by his visa's expiration. He wondered if he'd be welcomed by the Americans since the Vietnam War five years ago had left deep scars and many false stereotypes.

His mission would require many hurdles. As Xuan pondered his plans during his ride home, he was taken out of his thoughts when the vehicle came to a halt. "We've arrived, sir." The new place was located in an older quiet part of Houston's suburbs. As the old man pulled his luggage up the doorsteps, neighbors were peeping out their windows, wondering why a stranger had come. A couple passed by and Xuan bowed. Outside in front, he noticed the paint was peeling off. He opened the door and immediately took his belongings upstairs to the bedroom. Before going upstairs, he took out the folder with his mission's details and set it on the dining room table. Not minding the mess in the house, he sat down and opened it.

For Xuan, every day for the last five years since October 22nd, 1975 was a living hell. Inside the folder, were the profiles of seven American soldiers; seven decorated men who would pay dearly for the crime they had committed.

There were tough immigration screenings in order to come to the United States and many questions Xuan couldn't answer but somehow he made it through. With six months left, Xuan came to do what he only lived for. His good memories of his wife and daughter were fading away as the days passed by. Now that he's seventy years old, a combination of age and time were rapidly taking its toll. The old man knew he had to do something before it was too late.

His easiest target would be Tim Marshall; a fucking slob who was old and weak. Xuan had been trailing him and the other six through a Vietnamese friend in the US military for the last two years. He discovered that Tim was a regular at the local hospital in town but didn't know why.

"Bastard!" yelled Xuan as he stared at Tim's photo. Listed in his file were Tim's work address and social security number. By tracking his social, he'd get more information but that was a long shot. For now, Tim's workplace would do and it wouldn't be easy killing him inside there.

The next man was Ben Rogers; a wealthy Texan who owned land up and down the United States and had done quite well for himself financially after the War. Ben had three children and his second wife was half his age. He was spotted often playing at the most prestigious golf clubs around the country. Xuan wondered how he got so rich; growing up in a home with Jewish parents in the ghettos of Houston before he enlisted in the service.

Matthew Jones, the third man; a heavy gambler that lost his home and was now renting a one-bedroom apartment with his wife of twenty years. Matthew has weekly visits scheduled to see a psychiatrist, due to post-traumatic stress disorder.

Xuan then took a sip of tea, setting the three men's files aside and moving onto the next.

Zachary Hamilton served after Vietnam as the right hand of Major General Harris of the Texas

Brigade and was well respected amongst the townsmen and military.

As Xuan read further, his heart raced and decided to not to touch the remaining files for the rest of the day. He was ready to go on with his mission to find Tim and longed for the moment to begin tasting redemption.

Someone knocked on the door. Xuan carefully walked slowly towards it, peeking through the hole. A woman in her late forties was there smiling. "Who the fuck is this?" thought Xuan puzzled by this woman's smile. Yet, he opened.

"Hi, I saw you just moved here!"

"Yes, about an hour ago."

"Well, I wanted to welcome you to our little community." The woman then handed Xuan a box. Maybe its a bomb! A thought that crossed Xuan's mind because of its warmth.

"It's right out of the oven."

Xuan wasn't sure what to say. He was never given a welcoming gift from anyone back home.

"Thank you," said Xuan setting the box down on a stand near the door.

"I'm Katherine by the way. Nice to meet you." She offered her hand to shake.

"Xuan Lang." He said shaking hers.

"I'll see you around, and if you need anything, we're always a doorbell away."

She waved goodbye and left. Xuan smiled while shutting the door and returned to his seat, wondering what if someone else will come. The details surrounding the remaining men were vague and Xuan didn't even bother glancing further. He knew he'd catch each one of them sooner or later.

For the remainder of the afternoon, Xuan sipped on a few cups of green tea, reclining in a Lazyboy that the previous owners had left behind and watching the local news until nightfall came.

* * *

Two weeks passed and it was the night of Tim Marshall's birthday. Xuan devised a plan to slip in Tim's party as a waiter. Xuan purchased a black suit and a red tie for the occasion. The old man's slicked hair was too shiny from the mousse. In Texas, he noticed everyone wore cowboy hats but Xuan had forgotten to buy one.

Once the taxi arrived, Xuan got in and the driver asked during the ride, "Are you new here in town?", staring through the rear-view mirror.

"I just arrived this morning."

"Well, Houston's a lovely place. I'm sure you will grow fond of it."

"I hope so," said Xuan staring out the window, realizing that they were downtown from the towering lights of the buildings.

"We're here, sir."

"Thank you and keep the change."

"Thanks, sir. God bless."

Tim's party was held at a high-end restaurant called the Taste of Texas and it was already packed. Xuan made his way through the side exit to the kitchen. A few waiters looked at Xuan but continued working as he strolled past the chef's grill to the lobby.

Tim and his wife arrived a few minutes later, holding each other's hands. The guests made space for the couple and clapped for them as they came inside. Tim looked much older than the picture Xuan had in his file while his wife looked more like his daughter. Tim and his wife walked by Xuan and waved, thanking the guests for coming. Xuan looked for an empty seat at one of the tables and saw one with a group of couples seated. Just as Xuan was about to sit down, a man said, "Excuse me. This seat's already taken, bud."

"Just as I was about to introduce myself. I'm Xuan Lang." The couples looked at him, expecting him to leave.

"Never heard that name before."

A woman among them said, "Be nice fellas. He's obviously new to this town."

"So, are you here for the auction, Xuan or the birthday party?" asked a man opposite of Xuan.

"Auction or Birthday party? That's funny. I guess this is a gathering for the rich and famous." The table laughed at Xuan's response.

"What business do you have here in Texas, Xuan?" asked another man at the far end of the table.

"Herbs! I own an herb shop." This was partly true. Back in Vietnam, Xuan opened one, but was forced to close down when his family was killed. *This business might make money here. What an excellent idea!*

"And is this business of yours profitable?" a man asked as the others at the table laughed wildly.

"Why would I keep doing it if it wasn't?"

The man frowned at Xuan's sarcasm. "I see. Maybe we can talk about it more over dinner."

An hour passed and the hall's lights began dimming. Tim and his wife walked to the podium in the middle of the room.

"Finally, it's starting," a woman said clasping her hands. She was a close friend of Tim.

Xuan's eyes were fixed on Tim; studying his every

movement and largely ignoring the claps from the audience.

"Ladies, Gentleman." Tim grabbed the microphone as he waved. "I'm thrilled you all could join us tonight."

As Xuan listened, a group of men brought out some expensive paintings, one by one and some other valuables.

"We'll now begin," announced Tim's wife, smiling uncontrollably.

The crowd then became silent, waiting. Xuan had enough money to participate and thought it might be a way to start a friendship with Tim in order to get closer to the others.

"First up is the Marionette Vase from the 19th century," proclaimed Tim pointing. Xuan kept quiet as it wasn't something he didn't see value in.

"Eight hundred dollars!" Tim's wife's words echoed through the hall.

"Nine!" a woman yelled behind Xuan as her husband disapproved.

"Nine hundred dollars." Tim pointed at the woman.

"One thousand!" a voice from another table yelled.

"One thousand and two hundred!" another man quickly followed up.

"Pathetic. So much for an object with such little

importance!" A thought that crossed Xuan's mind as the bidding was taking place.

"Sold!" A woman in red hair cheered, clapping loudly.

Next up was a painting, which resembled something that Xuan's wife would have made. It brought back memories of the happier moments in his life and he couldn't let this reminder slip away.

"Starting at five hundred dollars."

"Six hundred!" one man yelled a few feet away from him.

"Seven hundred!" Xuan raised his hand.

Everybody turned their attention to the old Asian man; a new face in town.

The attention soon faded when another person bidded higher. "Nine hundred."

Xuan didn't think that this painting would be worth this much, but he continued. "One thousand."

No one else was willing to bid higher. Content with his possession, Xuan poured himself a glass of wine.

"Sold!" Tim announced.

Xuan raised his glass in thanks.

The auction continued on for another hour, and Xuan started conversing with the men and women at the table. Sadly, Xuan couldn't get close to Tim, even though he had his eyes on him for most of the evening.

"All the owners of tonight's auction who spent over $1,000, please come this way," announced Tim's wife.

Xuan got up and followed the others through a back door. He along with four others entered and waited until Tim's wife had arrived.

"Congratulations, ladies and gentlemen." The young woman introduced herself as Anna standing in front of the valuables.

She then ordered for the men to bring drinks. Anna noticed Xuan sitting by himself and walked over, "Excuse me, sir. You've chosen one of my dearest pieces."

Xuan almost choked wiping his mouth. His expression made her laugh. He set his glass down and said, "I'll be sure to cherish it."

"My husband forced me to sell it. We've been having financial problems lately." Anna paused. "Stupid me! I've shouldn't had said that."

"It's fine. We're all human and have financial problems sometimes in life." "Well, now I'm sure my little secret is safe with you."

"You have my word," smiled Xuan.

Tim's got financial problems, huh? Xuan thought as he pictured how he would use that weakness against him as Anna kept talking. Then their conversation was cut short by Tim who grabbed Anna by the waist and pulled her towards him.

"You must be the infamous Xuan Lang."

"That's right except for the infamous part."

"My wife and I would like to invite you to dinner tomorrow night. All winners are invited. It would be a shame if you didn't show up." Tim was looking more at his wife than Xuan.

"I'll think about it, but thank you for the offer."

"Please, do. You'll meet some great men and women in this town."

Tim didn't like men near his wife. She was young and busty and at times, flirtatious. Xuan got up and walked around, small-talking with the other bidders in the room. He knew he'd left a bad first impression with Tim who'd probably was thinking he was flirting with Anna.

XUAN WAS NOWHERE near being ready. His room was covered with clothes; feeling he didn't pack enough and decided to wear the suit he wore at the funeral of his family.

It reminded him of the mission that he had set out for. Five years ago, his wife was raped by the Americans officers; one being Vietnamese. They then murdered his daughter in cold blood lighting the house on fire. Xuan was out at work and came home heartbroken; seeing the men savagely destroy his life before his very eyes.

The Vietnam War left unbearable scars. Putting on this suit was one of many scars that Xuan Lang would always remember. The last time he wore it, he was reminded of his angels going to the heavens.

Sighing, he buttoned it up and straightened his

posture in front of the mirror. Tonight, Xuan knew he'd have to look presentable.

A taxi came by to take him to Tim's home. As they rode through the streets, Xuan thought about him not saying a word to his neighbors. It's been almost ten days since he arrived and he knew that they were watching him. They had to, simply for the fact that he was the only Asian in the neighborhood of military veteran families. Since there was heavy traffic, he knew he'd be at least fifteen minutes late. Tim and Anna didn't seem to mind and welcomed him telling him to come right in.

"We've been expecting you, Xuan." Anna embraced him as Tim looked on, jealous.

"Traffic was a nightmare! I'm sorry."

The house was a mansion, and it was strange that a person who had financial problems could afford living here.

There was jazz playing in the background and Xuan heard laughter. Xuan's breathing hitched when he spotted four men; all who were responsible for the death of his family. They were seated at a wooden table, laughing.

"Where are the other three?" thought Xuan referring to Joshua Warren, Ronald Ravens, and Duong Gian. Duong was an interpreter contracted by the US Marines and was the main culprit leading the rape of Xuan's wife as Xuan and his daughter watched.

"Please take a seat," said Anna breaking Xuan's thoughts. The feeling of seeing these men sent chills through the old man's body. He wanted to lunge and stab them to death but he had to remain calm and patient.

He sat in silence, listening to a few men who showed up for the special gathering but the bidders hadn't arrived yet. After a few refreshments and chatting with the guests, Tim and Anna finally joined everyone at the table, clicking their wine glasses to get everyone's attention. "Unfortunately, the buyers from last night's auction will not be able to join us today except for Mr. Xuan Lang. Fellas be nice as we'd like to say cheers for new friendships."

The men stopped talking and stood up.

"Cheers to that," a man by the name of Zachary spoke as the group laughed.

"Now, I hope our food appeases your taste buds. Anna tried her best here," said Tim as he hugged Anna.

Xuan didn't see Anna as serious. She was young and looked as if she was always out of the home perhaps with her girlfriends more than Tim.

"It smells delicious," said Ben staring at the food.

"Please, dig in gentleman," said Anna.

Xuan took a few slices of roast beef, mashed potatoes, and salad. When he took a bite, he was ready to spit it out. Anna's cooking was nowhere near complimentary. She should have hired a catering service instead. As Xuan ate, he had the urge to vomit, shutting his eyes to avoid its dullness.

"How do you like the food, Xuan?"

Tim looked at Xuan strangely as even he was having second thoughts about his wife's cooking.

"One of the best meals I've had in a while."

"I'm so flattered, you've just made my day, Xuan," giggled Anna as Tim watched her reaction.

Tim was a dick. After a few words with Anna, he cleared his throat. "Gentlemen, you haven't told me about what you've been working on lately." He turned his focus on the three cowards opposite to Xuan.

"Don't act as if you don't know, Tim. We've been struggling as of late with the new city ordinances, but I think we'll be open for business soon," said Matthew as he wiped his mouth with a cloth.

"What kind of company are you gentlemen springing up, if you don't mind me asking?" The men turned their attention to the old man as Anna stuffed herself, not wanting to be a part of the conversation.

"A new car dealership," said Zachary.

"That's smart. Do you think it could make big money out here?"

"Why wouldn't it? The roads are being improved daily and many are looking to buying new cars before a recession hits. Damn, Reagan is coming in office in a few months," said Matthew.

"I must admit there's still a lot of work to be done," added Zachary.

Xuan wasn't interested in anything they had to say but wanted to build a relationship to get closer to the men. As they chatted on, all of them had a different outlook on the business.

Then Zachary broke the ice, "That's why I have these two buds by my side," grinned Zachary as he hugged Matthew and Duong, pulling them tightly.

Xuan felt defeated by their happiness and wanted to change topics. "Hopefully, I'll find some friends as true as you before I die."

"I truly hope you do, my little Asian friend," answered Matthew sarcastically.

"By the way, I'm Xuan Lang."

"Where are you from?" asked Ben, seemingly curious by Xuan's name.

"I'm from the Philippines."

"What business do you have here in America?" probed Matthew.

"I'm opening an herb shop not too far from downtown." Xuan expected them to laugh.

"That's an unusual career for a man your age," said

Matthew. The men were maybe ten years younger, so it was funny how they looked down on the old man. *"Fucking Americans."* Xuan took another bite of the bland roast beef.

"It truly is but an old man has a passion for fixing people."

"Don't we all?" exclaimed Tim raising his glass as everyone followed.

Within an hour and a half, Xuan wrapped up the paperwork and took possession of his painting. Just as he was about to leave, Zachary came over to him, "Xuan, we'd be honored if you could spare us some of your time this week and go golfing with us."

"Why are you inviting me? You don't even know why I'm here." Xuan was thinking as Zachary spoke.

"We feel bad for treating you the way we did in the beginning. Our little town is not used to strangers. Since most of us come from military families, we have a code of honor. Please accept our apologies."

"Ok, I'll accept that and think about it."

* * *

The next morning, Xuan was awakened by loud

knocks. Xuan came downstairs in his pajamas and opened the door. Standing there, was his neighbor Katherine.

"Xuan, I didn't mean to wake you," Katherine said looking at Xuan puzzled.

"Oh no, Katherine, it's fine. How can I help you?" Xuan grabbed the handle of the door, resting on it.

"The owners couldn't get a hold of you yesterday," said Katherine taking out a folder.

"I've been pretty busy these days. Sorry!"

"Well, they said the house comes in a package deal with the store they own."

"A store? Why didn't they mention this before?" Xuan opened the door, inviting her inside. There were boxes of empty Chinese food on the table. "Sorry for the mess, I haven't had guests yet." He set a case to the side and directed her to the sofa.

"It's fine." Katherine opened the folder, taking out the papers. "The owners had a convenience store, but it failed miserably. Let's say they weren't keeping stock like they were supposed to."

Xuan wondered what happened as it looked like Katherine wasn't fond of them.

"Is the store nearby?"

"Yes, just down on the corner, but I have to admit that it needs some fixing." Katherine chuckled as she handed Xuan the folder. "You'll need to sign here and

I'll mail it to them. They are away on vacation in Maui for God knows how long." After reading over everything, Xuan signed off and handed the contract back. As Katherine was leaving, she left the remaining papers and keys to the store on the table.

Xuan retired close to five years ago from the army and opened his first business in selling herbs after the tragedy. He was given his pension and lived a simple life. However, fate played with him dearly. Countless times, he blamed God for his unfortunate happenings. He was a man destroyed by those who destroyed his family.

As Katherine closed the door, Xuan was anxious to know of the store's condition. He changed quickly and headed down the road, remembering Katherine's directions vaguely. As he walked, he almost started doubting her. "Maybe I'm on the wrong road?" After passing by a few stores, he saw some bold letters written on the front of a closed storefront reading - "Seamans." Xuan fumbled the keys while unlocking the door, excited about going inside.

He looked around, seeing the store was full of dust and cobwebs. "A free store but a lot of work," questioned the old man if this shop had a chance of turning a profit.

Xuan graduated from college in holistic medicine and knew almost every herb that existed. Slowly, a vision of how to set up the place was already being planted. What about the customers. Do they use holistic remedies? The location seemed perfect, and by it not having any pharmacies close by, the business could flourish.

There were boxes stacked up to the ceiling in the back storage room, almost tumbling over when Xuan opened the door. The area was smaller than the front but big enough to stock inventory. The paint on the wall was peeling off, but there were a sink and other appliances. Not being able to tolerate the mess any longer, Xuan started putting the boxes on top of one another and pushing them aside to one corner.

"Xuan!?"

Katherine's voice startled him, making him jump. She was holding plastic bags and from Xuan's conclusion, she'd just done grocery shopping.

"You scared me." He said, dusting off his hands.

"Sorry, I was passing by from the market and saw the door open. I didn't think you were coming here right away."

"Yeah, I wanted to give the place a good look. I

have time today." Xuan sat down on an old chair in the center of the room.

"I'm impressed. I thought you would leave it be and didn't want anything to do with it. For sure, you proved me wrong."

"How could I not?" Xuan stood up and walked Katherine to the front area, where an old cash register was left behind. "This could be put to use. If we can put a little muscle in this old shop, it would be nice," hinted Xuan

"You're right. It's an excellent idea opening an herbal shop yourself in this neighborhood. There are always sick people here. Many got ill when returning from the War," said Katherine following behind Xuan and looking around.

"I'm planning for just that. By the way, do they have this time of shop around here?"

"Oh my, no!" Katherine said, setting aside her bags. "And I'd be glad to spread the word about the business for you. I know everyone in this area."

"So, this sounds like a partnership?" laughed Xuan.

"I guess so. Where should I start?" She rolled up her sleeves, placing her hands on her hips, ready.

"There is a lot of dirt," said Xuan pointing to the floor. "We can start here. Let me pay for some supplies."

"No, no. I have enough at home." Katherine went

home and brought the supplies back and Xuan realized it would be a longer day than usual.

Xuan began cleaning what he could until Katherine returned. The plumbing wasn't working properly in the back as the sink clogged. After many attempts to unclog it, Xuan sighed, "This is useless," sitting down on one of the stools and wiping his forehead. The shop's bell chimed and Katherine walked in, donning a pair of gloves, fully ready.

"Isn't this a bit over the top?" asked Xuan.

"Not at all, have you seen this place?" She set a bucket down, placing her hands on her hips while looking around.

"It's not as bad as you think it is. You'll see, partner." She started by dumping the boxes, one by one outside. Then, she went to the storage shelves, clearing out the outdated cans of food and other rubbish. Xuan had the easiest chore, sweeping the rooms and putting trash from Katherine in the dumpster.

After four hours, they finished and Xuan was tired even though he didn't work as hard. He invited Katherine over for coffee which she did after bathing. She told Xuan she was a nurse at the local hospital and had two children in college. Her new husband's a bank accountant who's barely home and always away. Xuan then told her about his family back in Vietnam. Before midnight, Katherine had left. Xuan saw Katherine as a nice person to have as a partner but knew not to trust her with his mission. Then, he sat regretting about allowing her to get close to him. The old man vowed not to let anyone inside.

Xuan didn't know whether to accept Tim's invitation to go golfing or not. Inside, he came up with many excuses. He never wanted to see their faces again, but he must. Xuan was confused, realizing that he had no gear for the occasion. The only thing that resembled golf in his possession was a green polo shirt. When his phone rang in the wee hours of the morning, it caught the old man off-guard. He stumbled down the staircase to hurry and answer it.

"Hello?"

"Xuan?"

"Who's this?" Xuan knew who it was.

"Zachary." How the hell did he get my number?

"I'm calling to make sure if you're coming tonight at six, pal?"

Xuan cleared his throat after a long silence. "Yeah, sure. Why at six? Isn't it late?"

"Bud, golf is fun at night. Believe me, you'll see."

"If you say so."

"All right, I'll see you at the Walden. Don't forget —" added Zachary.

Before he hung up, Xuan asked, "Wait, how did you get my number?"

"I got it from Tim. He has your information from the auction, remember?"

Xuan never thought Tim would give his contact information. "I see. Thanks, see you later, Zach." Xuan ran back upstairs to his closet, raging inside. Furthermore, he didn't have a precise plan on how he was going to kill all seven. He put on his shirt and would leave everything else to the guys.

The 6 o'clock hour came quickly and the weather outside was warm and mild. Xuan didn't have any emotion about meeting his least favored individuals. Now, it feels like he's sleeping with the enemy.

The Walden Golf Club was only a few miles away. By the looks of the outside, it was sealed off from the public. Xuan fastened his duffle bag over his shoulder and walked inside. The reception was high-end and the ceiling had pictures engraved of some of the world's most famous golfers. The staff greeted everyone warmly and the old man didn't have a clue where he was headed. How would Zachary know I arrived? He stood close by the receptionist desk, patiently waiting.

For close to fifteen minutes, many passed by, all

wearing polo shirts and white shorts. They matched the people he saw on an American show called "The Loveboat," but its subtitles were in Vietnamese. As the old man started drifting away in thought, a voice startled him.

"Xuan!"

"Xuan!"

Xuan turned, seeing seven men coming to the reception area; Joshua, Ronald, Ben, Matthew, Tim, Zachary, and Duong Gian.

He was taken aback by their presence, tumbling back as the striking memory of his family's murder resurfaced. Those men have no shame and didn't know Xuan was here to settle the score once and for all. No one knew what these cowards had done, and Xuan Lang was planning on exposing all.

"Good day, gentlemen." Xuan held out his hand to shake theirs.

"Are you ready?" chuckled Zachary.

The others laughed, probably because of Xuan's outfit. They were dressed in white pants and blue polo shirts. A few of them were wearing USA caps and it was hilarious. "You all may be dressed like Arnold Palmer, but I have what it takes to beat you." The joke was corny, but the men grinned.

"Nice one, Xuan," said Matthew, grabbing him on

the shoulder. "My new Asian friend, Xuan Lang. You've met Tim of course, Ben and Zachary."

As Matthew introduced him to the others, Xuan looked at them straight in the eye. There was no backing down now. This was a dangerous game, and the seven criminals were the players.

"Joshua Warren." The man had blonde hair and bright blue eyes. By his looks, he seemed unfriendly as if he was having a bad day.

Xuan continued to the second one on his left.

"I'm Ronald Ravens." Ronald took both Xuan's hands trying to mimic an Asian salute of some sort. He had a wrinkled face and seemed kind.

Xuan had second thoughts on turning to the last. "Duong Gian. I think we met a few days ago. You're from the Philippines, right?"

"Oh, oh yes! We sure did," stuttered Xuan.

Right away, Xuan recognized Duoug's accent.

"This way," Tim stated, walking to the sliding doors of the patio. Tim and Ben carried the golf balls while the caddies took the clubs and rest of the equipment. Ronald held the keys to the golf carts. The group of men followed behind and saw the golf course light up from a distance, contrasting the dusk.

Xuan stared in awe at the beautiful view while the others had seen it many times before. After walking down a long set of stairs to the area of the golf carts,

Xuan jumped inside with Joshua, Zachary, and Tim. The others paired up and drove ahead.

The endless terrain of the green was reeling leaving Xuan in a trance. The warmness of the evening sun was getting the better of him. It started becoming hotter than the daylight and Xuan knew it was his blood boiling. As they neared their portion of the course, Xuan started imagining where these guys learned how to play.

"Do you know how to golf, Xuan?" yelled Tim from the front seat.

"Honestly, I do not, but I'll learn from you, guys tonight."

"So, you won't beat us after all. Bud, It's easy. All you have to do is put the ball in the hole." Tim and Zachary chuckled at Joshua's description.

"It's settled then; I'm good at that."

The men roared like wild animals and Xuan wasn't impressed.

The cart came to a sudden screech, and everyone jumped out. "Finally, we get to have a rematch," shouted Ben from the other side. Then they gathered in a circle to divide the teams into fours while the caddies prepared the course.

"I think we should split up like before since we already know who's with whom. We'll take Xuan," uttered Matthew.

Xuan believed they would surely lose now. He wasn't good at sports.

"I see you're lucky." Duong came beside Xuan.

"Let the best team win, fellas," yelled Ben.

"You're first dickheads," taunted Tim. Xuan was grouped with Matthew, Tim, and Joshua while Ronald, Duong, Ben, and Zachary were the challengers.

Eighteen holes of golf will make it a long evening. Ronald had hired some college-women caddies to spark up things. Ben was the first one to start. Setting the golf ball on the tee and gripping the club tightly, he focused on his swing while sweating profusely.

Ben hit the ball and it landed near to the hole, almost going in. The caddies clapped and kissed Ben as his teammates cheered him on.

"I see you got better than the last time," mocked Joshua.

They continued, taking turns until it was Xuan's. His team gave him instructions while the opposing team mimicked the way he clutched the golf club. Xuan calculated the distance from the ball to the hole almost resembling a professional. When he swung, the golf ball flew across a little left of his target but close enough for a bogey.

His teammates clapped, surprised at the old man. Zachary whistled, taunting Xuan. "So many fake people," thought Xuan. Now, it was time to focus on getting the ball inside the hole. Xuan walked to the spot with the caddies, measuring the distance mentally as he approached. He then swung, resulting the ball going inside the hole. Everyone cheered and one of the caddies hugged Xuan while kissing him on the cheek. The guys laughed, seeing Xuan uneasiness.

"Cheer up, bud. The girl likes you," said Matthew.

"Not my cup of tea."

"Haha."

Now, it was Tim's turn. Xuan didn't pay much attention, tuning into Duong and Joshua's conversation. Xuan walked over to join in.

"I already started the shipment and it will reach Vietnam in about two to three days, tops." Duong lowered his voice as he saw Xuan approaching. They cleared their throats when he walked up.

"Gentlemen. I'm impressed. An amazing job for an old hag, am I right?" joked Xuan about himself, causing them to laugh. While the others played, the three began chatting.

"Don't joke around like that, Xuan. We are honorable military men. There is no pride. This is a friendly game of golf. We've allowed you in our little circle. Be a little bit more humble." Duong saw the seriousness of Joshua while Xuan was clearly puzzled.

"Hey man, I'm kidding." All three burst in laughter.

"You know I was about to kill you," returned Xuan giggling.

"I bet you were," joked Joshua.

"Duong!" Ben called. "It's your turn, you fucking cunt."

The men and the caddies started moving to the next hole and Duong was excited to show what he could do. He put on a show, striking the ball right in the hole without hesitation. Surely, Duong played this game many times before as it appeared he was the best player in the group.

Everyone clapped, and within the next two hours, they were at the last hole. Tired and sweaty, the sun had already started set. The match was thrilling, but for Xuan, he couldn't wait to go.

Tim was the last to go, and to the team's dismay, it ended it with a total error, leaving Duong's team to win. Xuan's first target, Tim was sad and the old man put his arm around him to comfort him.

After the match, Tim invited Xuan for a drink at his

house and as much as he didn't want to go, he came along.

When they pulled up to Tim's, Tim noticed his living room's lights were dimmed and Anna's car was parked in the garage. "Lord, this woman will want to talk all night," thought Tim. They rang the doorbell and waited for his wife to answer. "Why doesn't he have the key? Strange!" thought Xuan. She didn't answer but there was some bustle coming from behind the door. Someone was inside. Tim banged on the door nonstop.

"Anna! Open up right now or I'll fucking kill you!" When she didn't, Tim kicked the door down and stared.

His wife was half naked while a young man was climbing out of the kitchen window, naked with his clothes in his hands. She froze at the sight of Tim and Xuan. Tim ran to the kitchen, pushing Anna down to the ground and out of the way to catch the guy, but he was gone.

"What the fuck have you done?"

"Tim, please I can explain." Anna picked up the leftover pieces of clothing off the couch. Xuan watched, started.

"You have nothing to explain. Save yourself the humiliation. How could the fuck could you do this to me?" Tim's voice was cracked and he was about to cry.

Xuan couldn't believe this was playing out like a movie.

"He is just a co-worker. We were—"

"I don't care who he is. This is my house, and you don't get to disrespect me like this." He pointed around. "Get your stuff and get the fuck out now! I'll be having my lawyer write up the divorce papers in the morning."

Tim sat on the couch; the same one Anna had been making out on. Xuan remained standing, not knowing what to do or say. Xuan partly smiled, knowing Tim had it coming.

Anna came down the stairs, with her mascara smeared down her eyes from her crying. "I love you, Tim." Those were her last words.

The scene worsened when Tim started weeping. Xuan had no choice but to comfort him. "Kill him now! Frame Anna" imagined Xuan.

"Listen, it will get better." Tim didn't respond, resting his head on his hands, breathing out wearily.

"It won't, Xuan. She's the only woman I love more than my own life."

"Women like her don't deserve your love, Tim. I'm sure you'll find someone worthy." The night's winds rushed inside from door being left open and Xuan got up to shut it.

The night passed as Tim kept crying over Anna

while Xuan patiently listened. Xuan excused himself to use the restroom. He sneaked into Tim's bedroom, opened his drawers, spotting papers of bank transfers and receipts to Anna. Tim had spent a fortune on jewelry, rental cars, and hair appointments for her. Xuan remembered Anna talking about their money problems and she was responsible for them.

Xuan came back downstairs, finding Tim in the same spot. His vulnerability was to Xuan's advantage and killing him would be easier than the old man thought.

"Tim, I'm sorry bud, but I have to go. I have work in the morning." Tim escorted Xuan to the door and didn't say a single word.

"Take it easy, Bud. I'll check on you tomorrow."

Xuan finished planning for his first kill - Tim Marshall. It would be harder than expected since Tim was working long hours trying to forget about Anna. Two weeks had passed since Xuan had last seen Tim. Tim called Xuan yesterday, inviting him to hang out after work, and told him to meet him at his job at five. Xuan told Tim if he wasn't there by 5, he'd have to reschedule due to a large shipment of herbs coming in.

Earlier in the week, Xuan got his firearm license in the mail. The old man had no problems getting one now that he's running a business. Texas' gun laws were so lax he only had to show a copy of the renter's contract for the store. Xuan needed only one gun to finish off what he came to America for.

Xuan studied the revolver, a Baretta 92F, lying on the table. He was ready and as he put on his coat, the doorbell sounded. It was Katherine. Xuan placed the gun in his coat pocket and proceed to the door.

"Xuan, sorry to bother you. May I ask a favor?"

"Yes, sure."

"My youngest is over for the weekend, and his temperature isn't going down."

"Give me a minute and I'll be right out."

"Ok."

Xuan closed the door, took out the gun and it, then placed it in a flowerpot nearby and came outside. Katherine hurried as Xuan had never seen her like this before. They reached her home and proceeded to her son's room at the far end of the hallway. He was laying in bed, scarcely breathing and sweating heavily.

"I gave him medicine this morning, but his temperature isn't dropping. From what I see, he has a high fever." Katherine gave Xuan a plastic chair and the old man looked over the young man. The scene reminded Xuan of his wife, Binh whenever she was sick. The old man deeply reflected as he closely monitored Katherine's son.

"I have some herbs that may help." Katherine handed Xuan a plastic bag in which he saw White Willow. That herb was discovered thousands of years ago by Chinese doctors and oddly, Katherine had them.

"You'll need to make him tea with this White

Willow." Xuan handed her the herb, and Katherine rushed to the kitchen. After finding Yarrow inside the bag also, he joined Katherine to make another treatment. Xuan took elderflower, peppermint, boneset, cayenne, and ginger from Katherines's counter and told her it would be the perfect blend. Katherine finished making the first blend and rushed back. Xuan came inside minutes later, giving the young man his medicine and watched his response as the young man's sweat began to decrease. Katherine jumped up in joy, embracing Xuan. Then, Xuan excused himself, as he was a man on a mission.

Xuan scouted the area before Tim left from work, discovering an alleyway nearby. It would be the ideal place to execute Tim with nothing but junkies' things left behind. Waiting outside, Xuan watched the workers as they left for the day. His leather jacket didn't stop the fall's wind from entering. As the clock reached 5:10, Xuan wondered if Tim was bullshitting him. The old man arrived over two hours ago, so another a few minutes wouldn't hurt.

A little boy came up to Xuan, selling a newspaper, and he kindly declined. "I'm sorry." Subsequently, Tim came to the front entrance, looking disturbed. His hair was rumpled, and his shirt was half-open. His troubled expression stood out as he walked slowly, often looking behind as if he was expecting something bad to happen. Xuan was waiting far enough that Tim couldn't spot him. It was 5:32 and Xuan already gave him a heads-up about not coming. The only thing Xuan wanted was for Tim to walk through that alley. The pistol felt cold against the old man's skin. It would be his first murder, and he felt high-strung.

Tim turned down another block, catching Xuan off-guard, as the old man almost collided into a pole. The sound caught Tim's attention, and Xuan quickly hid behind a dumpster. The moment was getting close as Tim getting closer to that alleyway. Xuan checked the surroundings and there was no one in sight. The streets were almost empty, making an escape fairly easy. He then ran up to Tim from behind. The old man pulled out the Baretta and aimed; the cold barrel pressed up against the back of Tim's head made him stop. Tim placed his hands in the air thinking someone was robbing him. Xuan smiled speculating about this bastard's final seconds.

Tim turned around and his eyes widened. "What are you doing, Xuan?" Xuan didn't immediately answer. Two worlds collided in the strangest of manners and yet it will be ashes to ashes, dust to dust for one.

"It's time to pay for what you've done." Xuan's voice shivered violently, ignoring Tim's endless sobs. Tim pleaded to Xuan why was he doing this.

"My wife, my daughter." Xuan pulled out two photos, holding them up. Tim was at a loss of words. He remembered and felt ashamed. Tim's weeping only grew louder.

"What do you have to say, you fucking bastard before I kill you?" yelled Xuan regretting he hadn't already done so.

"I'm sorry, please don't." Tim dropped to his knees, crying. "We were drunk fucks. Ok? It wasn't my fault." Xuan stood there shaking his head in disbelief.

"Well, this is mine." Xuan shot Tim in the head. His body slammed on the cold ground and the old man stared, relishing the display of blood pouring. He knew Houston's news stations would be flooded with the death of their decorated marine, Tim Marshall. Xuan promised himself the other executions would be more extreme.

Two days had passed since Tim Marshall's death and Xuan was walking through the Galleria looking for a gift for Katherine's son. He thought about buying a watch but had trouble finding a good one.

The Galleria was packed, and Xuan had already been to his third watch store. On the top floor, he spotted a decent jewelry store. A gentleman was wrapping up with a customer when an old lady came from behind the counter. "Hi, how can I help you today?" "Can you show me your best watch? I've looked around and haven't seen anything good yet."

"Sir. why of course." The lady smiled and went behind the counter, pulling out a black box. "This is my favorite. I'm sure it will tickle your fancy." She brought a Gold Seiko with a slick black leather band. Xuan looked at it for a long time, knowing the young man would like it. He wasn't easily defeated by an illness like his daughter.

The woman gift-wrapped the watch and the old man felt happy for once. He even strolled around the mall for a few hours before heading to Katherine's. She'd invited him over for dinner at seven, and now it was close to six. Xuan wanted to look presentable, so he bought himself an outfit at the mall.

Tim Marshall's funeral was held earlier in the day and Xuan excused himself, offering his deepest condolences. Joshua called Xuan the night before and Xuan acted shocked by Tim's passing. Xuan was arrived back home around 6:30 and after getting dressed, went downstairs to watch the news. The news coverage had a picture of Tim in the military and a quote enveloped in an American banner. The news reporter mentioned police were still searching for his killer and asked for the public's help in doing so. "Why is Tim's death getting so much coverage? He was an auctioneer overpricing his pieces of shit," shouted Xuan.

The news anchor kept sobbing as if she knew Tim personally. "Tim Marshall was Houston's face of auctions for years. We will forever remember his bid calling. It's a shame his life ended so violently." Xuan turned the TV off, not wanting to hear anymore. Whatever they know about Tim, was a lie. The man was wicked, and he deserved it.

Xuan left to go to Katherine's house and for the first time, he greeted his neighbors. They were baffled seeing an Asian man in their area.

Xuan rang Katherine's doorbell twice and she opened the door, embracing him in a hug. "Come inside, please." Xuan smelled the food as soon as he walked in. It seemed Katherine cooked better than Anna.

"Make yourself at home. My son Ethan will be down shortly." Katherine touched Xuan and he smiled. "Is she flirting with me?"

"Tell him to hurry. I have something for him," said Xuan holding up a bag.

"You shouldn't have. That boy has everything."

Katherine to go back to the kitchen and Xuan sat in the living room. To him, it was strange how American families were when getting to know them. Unlike the many Americans in Vietnam who were going around looking for prostitutes and drugs. As Xuan meditated, Katherine's son entered, introducing himself.

"Good day sir. I'm Ethan." The young man bowed respectfully surprising Xuan.

"Ethan, I'm Xuan. It's a pleasure to meet you in better spirits." Xuan urged him to sit down beside him. "Are you feeling better?"

Ethan was puzzled this strange man was asking about his condition. Xuan realized Ethan didn't recognize him from the other day.

"You had a fever the other day. Your mother and I helped take it away."

"Oh yes, sir. Thank you for the herbs. I feel much better now."

Xuan reached into his bag and took out the black box. "Call me Xuan." Ethan smiled as the old man handed the box to him.

Before Ethan opened it, Katherine walked in carrying plates of food; roast beef with gravy, mashed potatoes, salad, and corn on the cob.

"Hopefully, you'll enjoy this. It took my whole day and I need a new oven," said Katherine wiping the sweat off her forehead. Xuan valued her time even if the food would taste bad. Judging from the smell, it would be better than Anna's.

"You deserve a cooking award, Mom," laughed Ethan, forgetting to say grace while eating.

Katherine slapped him in back of the head. "The guest goes first and what about grace, dear. You remember?"

Ethan froze staring at Xuan, disappointed. "Yes, mom. I'm sorry."

"Now say grace and let's eat."

Katherine joined them after getting a few cups from the kitchen.

Xuan praised Katherine repeatedly as the three entertained in lengthy conversations, forgetting about their concerns. He learned a lot about Ethan and saw many similarities between the young man and his daughter, Binh. Suddenly, a hope sparked in him to spend time with the young man. Reasonably, as a way to fill the gap in Xuan's heart. He envisioned Binh looking down on him happily.

"So, Xuan," asked Ethan. "Why did you move to Texas?"

"Ethan, I think we should draw the line there and give Xuan privacy," stated Katherine.

Ethan lowered his head. "Sorry again, mom."

"It's okay," Xuan reassured Katherine. "I wanted to open my herb business in America. It will be good for Americans to experience different sorts of healing." Xuan answer was complex but enough for Ethan to comprehend.

"I'm curious about these herbs' ability to treat. Are they better than our medicines?" asked Ethan.

Xuan took a sip. "I wondered that too when I was your age, young man. My mother always had many herbs laying around our kitchen, and I grew interested. Little did I know, I would become an herbal expert later in life."

Ethan and Katherine laughed as the spirit in the house felt calm.

"I wonder, now that summer is almost here. Would you have a job opening at your store?" asked Ethan. Clearly, it was the last thing Xuan expected to hear. Many teens focused on school in Vietnam until graduation and did little odd jobs if they weren't.

"Ethan," warned Katherine, playing with her food. She was afraid her son was annoying Xuan.

"I've been looking for someone since your mom did all the work with fixing everything and we're now partners. I think your hands could do me some good." Xuan gave him a handshake agreement and Ethan accepted.

"Thank you, Xuan. It's such an honor." Then,

Katherine warned Ethan if he didn't listen to Xuan, she'd send him back home to his father for the summer. After supper, they played cards and Xuan lost every match. Ethan was winning and Katherine accused him of cheating. It was fun ever for Xuan.

"I have to excuse myself. I'm feeling a bit tired."

"Ok, Xuan. Thanks for coming." Katherine and Ethan then walked Xuan to the door.

"Oh! Before I forget. Ethan, come on Saturday for your first day of work."

It was Ethan's first day, and he was more excited he was out of college than starting work. The young man was top of his class, and Xuan respected that. Ethan might have had a girlfriend but didn't reveal much.

"Where should I place this, Xuan?" he asked while unpacking a big box filled with commodities.

"Line them up on the shelves. It'll look like we have many things for sale. Don't you agree?"

"I do."

While Ethan was stacking the items, in came Xuan's first customer; a middle-aged man, who seemed worried. "Do you need help with anything, sir?"

"Do you have any rosemary and chamomile?" The

man went in his pockets, taking out a few coins. Xuan knew he was poor and it saddened him. "Sure, sir."

Ethan helped, and the man asked the price, counting his coins.

"Your total is two dollars but—" paused Xuan as the man went to give him the money.

"It's on me."

Ethan packed the herbs and gave them to the man who smiled thanking them.

After the man left, Ethan had nothing but praises for Xuan. "We must help when we have it," remarked Xuan.

Xuan went to the back and picked out one of the newspapers from the heap of mail at the door. Reading the front-page, it took him by surprise when he saw Tim's widow's interview mentioned on Page 3. She talked about Tim, telling that their marriage was the best time of her life and how she couldn't imagine living without him. "Such lies," Xuan deemed. The old man shook his head and turned the page.

The day went by quickly with Xuan was tallying up the inventory in the back. Ethan didn't bother Xuan as he was needed out front. When Xuan and Ethan were ready to leave for the evening, a man was waiting outside the door, startling Ethan.

"Zachary!?"

"I was the man but not no more. Oh God! Tim's

gone." His words slurred as it appeared Tim had been drinking.

Xuan told Ethan to go, telling him the guy was a companion. "Ok, Xuan. See you tomorrow." Xuan tucked the shop's keys in his pocket while he walked over to Zachary. "What the hell are you doing here?" asked Xuan. Zachary stumbled with his face landing in Xuan's chest. Xuan pushed him away but It was clear Zachary was too drunk to walk. A car rode by seeing Zachary and the driver shouted his name but he didn't stop.

Xuan had no plans of killing him yet. He could have just left him on the sidewalk but Xuan carried Zachary to his house. He laid Zach down on his couch, hearing his heavy breathing that rocked the living room. The smell of alcohol scented the entire downstairs.

"Tim's gone and now others are alone." Zachary's words caught Xuan's attention as he took his shoes off, kicking them aside.

"What do you mean?"

"They think someone is after them after all these years. It's probably because it's—" Zachary's words stopped. He dozed off asleep. The only thing stopping the old man was Ethan who saw Zach and could implicate Xuan being the last person to be with him. Xuan went through Zachary's belongings and found only curled up dollars. He let Zach sleep in peace; a word that shouldn't be associated with this monster. Xuan went upstairs and knew he would gather more in the morning when Zachary was sober.

It was morning and Xuan Lang couldn't sleep well because of Zachary who was still asleep. Xuan went downstairs to wake him; stomping loud on the wooden steps. Xuan sensed Zach's loud snoring disturbed his neighbors. The old man cleared his throat at the bottom of the stairs, waking Zachary who jumped up in fear.

"Morning, Zach." Zachary rubbed his eyes while coughing.

"Xuan." Zachary hesitated, straightening himself up. Xuan came for one reason; a confession resulting from last night.

"I must've crashed here. Huh?" said Zachary tripping over his shoes.

"You did and coming to my shop drunk wasn't a good sign of faith. You scared my worker." Zachary couldn't look up at Xuan. "I'm sorry, bud."

"It's okay, but while we were chatting, you fell asleep saying something. What's happening to us?"

"I don't know where to even start, Xuan?" Zachary covered his face, plopping on the couch.

"Tim and I had a secret business involving gold. Tim had his own venture in the auction business, so this was a little extra on the side. We didn't mean to invest much, but as time went on, we were forced to." Xuan got up and brought Zach a glass of water.

"I stopped paying my share for a few months and the business failed." Zachary then began to cry.

"So what happened after that, Zach?"

"We borrowed from a loan shark, and now Tim's gone, they are after me."

"So they're following you?" Xuan wasn't sold on Zachary's story.

"Are you fucking kidding me? Of course, they are. They chased me around town yesterday. I'm lucky I survived."

"So, what to do now, Zach?" Xuan was worried the men might finish Zachary before he did. "Are they professionals?"

"I don't know, Xuan. I need your help."

"Tell me more about these people."

CHAPTER FOUR_

THE RAIN WAS POURING and Xuan was in downtown Houston with Zachary. They were pushed back and forth on the crowded sidewalks as they searched for a building that Zach said belonged to the loan sharks.

"This is it, Xuan."

Who would've thought Xuan Lang would be helping his enemy?

"What are we waiting for? Go inside." Zachary walked up the long set of steps as Xuan's heartbeat was racing.

"Should we go in, or wait for him to come out?"

Xuan couldn't believe how inexperienced Zach was. Xuan tapped on the door and no one answered, so he went in and Zach trailed behind. Down the long corridor, every door had numbers and letters with no names written.

"Now what?" whispered Zachary.

"Are we in the right building?"

"Number Seven A." Zachary spotted the door afar. "In our contract, they wrote this room as the address"

Xuan hurried to the door, tapping hard. While they waited, Zachary bit his fingernails.

"Come in." They went inside. There was a mahogany desk and with an older man in a cowboy hat seated.

"Good afternoon, Sir," expressed Zachary. The man stared while Xuan didn't say anything.

"May I help you?"

"I'm Zachary Hamilton. I'm sure you're familiar with my late partner, Tim Marshall."

Xuan interrupted, "Let's cut to the chase. Tim Marshall and my friend here took a loan from you and it seems you're making a mistake by taking it out on my friend here."

"My name is William Sage and it's a pleasure to meet you, now you may sit." William ignored Xuan. Zachary sat playing with his fingers and Xuan looked on.

"Sadly, I'm aware of Tim's death but your friend, Zachary was his business partner. It's suitable to say Zachary must pay off his debts." William rested his arms on the desk staring at Xuan.

"I'm struggling now. My wife just got fired, and

we're only surviving on my retirement," pleaded Zachary. Xuan kicked Zachary which him off guard. Xuan thought he was giving this man too much information.

"You're in debt, Mr. Zachary. Am I not clear when I say you must pay me back?" William was becoming annoyed while Xuan kept his cool.

"I know but all I need is a favor."

"What is it? I'm not in the business of giving favors," sighed William.

"I need more time. At least six months."

"Are you fucking insane?" William stood up and hit the desk. It was a sight worth seeing as the man looked like he was having a temper tantrum. "You better have my money on this desk in two months, Hamilton, or else I will send you my boys over to give you a pleasant going-away party." William pulled a pistol out of his drawer and placed it in front of him.

"That will certainly do, Mr. Sage. Thank you," Xuan excused himself while pulling Zachary.

Xuan didn't care except he should be the one to kill Zach. Zachary's debt wouldn't matter because he would be gone off the Earth before the deadline.

"It looked like I was the one doing all the negotiating and saved your life," said Xuan.

"You don't know, William. Tim used to tell me bad things about the guy."

"Like?" Xuan was speeding up to Zachary who was petrified.

"Not only did William take the life of someone who owed him, but he also destroyed the man's family by suing him afterward. Now, they are all living on the streets in the fucking ghetto. The wife is a crackhead and his children has been in and out of foster care."

"So, William Sage is the devil," grinned Xuan.

"The devil himself has a better face. I really hope Tim's now resting in heaven."

Xuan almost choked, hearing him.' "I hope you're right, Zach," said the old man sneeringly.

Xuan didn't have an exact plan on how to kill Zach, but he'll do it in joy. The old man turned on the radio to listen to the news hearing the weather report in the coming days. Xuan's isolation drained his spirits; seeing his daughter and wife running around the kitchen making his favorite dish.

Only if he'd stay home that day; it was the mistake that changed his life forever. The Americans were going back to their country that day, but seven cowards showed up to his home and came across his wife and daughter preparing him dinner. They were having fun with their corpses when they dumped into the basement like old rags. The horrifying sight of their dismembered bodies haunted Xuan by the day.

The Banh Mi was almost ready as Xuan snapped out of thoughts. He pondered whether to call Katherine and Ethan over. When he decided to do so, the doorbell rang. Messy, he opened it and it was Ethan, frightened.

"What's wrong?"

"There's a woman at the shop, going crazy, throwing stuff all around." The young man was breathing as if he ran for his life. Xuan listened realizing he still was dressed in his bedrobe but didn't care.

As they got closer to the shop, they heard Anna, Tim's wife cursing. "Oh my God! She knows," conceived Xuan.

"Go home, Ethan. I'll deal with this woman. Her husband just passed away," Xuan patted Ethan and entered the shop.

"You!" Anna rushed towards Xuan, hitting him. "You killed Tim. You fucking bastard!"

"Calm down, woman." Xuan held her wrists tightly. It was the least he could do. "Your husband is one of seven responsible for the deaths of my wife and daughter."

Anna took a few steps back, looking at Xuan.

"What, what do you fucking mean?"

"Tim with six other Marines raped my wife and

daughter and burnt their bodies. They tossed the corpses in my basement in Vietnam."

"No, no. Why would my Tim do that? You're lying. My Tim wouldn't do such a thing. Oh, God!"

"They did it, Anna. Many Americans have done bad things to our people." Xuan sat facing Anna. "Believe me, Anna. I have no choice."

"I should report you to the fucking police."

"You wouldn't do that, because it would mean I'd have to get rid of you, too. You know I could have set you up when you left Tim that evening. Instead, I had to hear his fucking sob story all night."

Anna was baffled and didn't move an inch. "So what's your plan now?"

"Wouldn't you want to know?" Xuan circled her, not yet giving her the pleasure of emotion.

She gulped, watching him, scared for her life.

Xuan kept staring and stayed silent.

"Then, I'll keep this our little secret under one condition," said Anna.

"I'm listening." Anna cleared her throat.

"You need to tell me, what other businesses Tim had. I need some money fast."

"I may consider it."

After Anna left, Xuan went directly to Katherine's house, to make sure Ethan was okay. Katherine was surprised to see Xuan in his robe and invited him in.

"I'm sorry to bother you, Katherine but I came by to tell Ethan I took care of our little problem at the shop."

Ethan suddenly came as Xuan was speaking.

"No worries, I took care of the problem. An old friend who's husband passed away. She needed some money and is possibly on drugs."

"May I get you a cup of tea?" asked Katherine.

"One cup wouldn't harm." Xuan sat as Ethan came, too.

"So who was that woman?" asked Ethan.

"A homeless person looking for food now that her husband had passed away."

"We should have called the police."

"I agree, but it's too late now. The woman is gone." Xuan looked down at his feet as he spoke.

"It's a shame we don't have a security camera," said Ethan.

"I'll get one from Highlands," smiled Xuan promising it wouldn't happen again.

"Tomorrow is my day off, but I'll come by to fix the mess she made."

"No need, Ethan. I'll clean it up."

"No offense, Xuan but I think you'll be tired after moving the second box," chuckled Ethan.

"Ethan! Watch your mouth," yelled Katherine from the kitchen.

"Maybe you're right, but I'll manage."

Katherine entered the room with two cups of tea and set it down. Xuan thanked her. "You've done well, Katherine."

"Glad you like it," smiled Katherine.

"I've been craving for some good tea."

"Ethan doesn't like it, but I drink it every morning." She took a sip not breaking eye contact. Katherine was attractive, but Xuan couldn't see her more than a friend. Even after his wife's death, Xuan was faithful even if it meant being alone for the rest of his life. His wife's memory would never be forgotten.

No one bothered to visit Xuan except Katherine and Ethan. Maybe they feared him. In the War, many Houston residents had lost relatives. Xuan knew this but he lost more than them.

"I'm afraid I have to go. My friends are waiting for me at the diner," said Ethan.

"I'll be leaving as well. My meal has probably over-cooked." Xuan got up, smiling.

"No need to leave, Xuan. This is your home, too."

"Maybe some other time. I promise."

Ethan and Xuan left out together and Xuan's Banh

Mi had overcooked, so he threw it away. When he finished cleaning, his phone rang.

"Let's meet tomorrow, Xuan." It was Zachary. "We'll be at the Crown Restaurant around noon." Zachary's tone was dispirited.

"I'm not sure if I'll be able to make it." He didn't want to meet with them yet and needed time to plan his second kill.

"You need to be here. Joshua will be coming too."

"I'll think about it. I don't understand why it's important. We're still grieving over Tim."

"Well, it is about Tim's death. We've hired a private investigator to look into the matter. The police aren't doing their fucking jobs fast enough."

"Okay. Give me a minute, so I can get a pen."

"Lion Square, 10796 Bellaire Blvd. Not far from you."

"Thanks."

The alarm clock interrupted Xuan from a night full of pleasant dreams about his family. He got up and cooked some new Bánh mì. While doing so, the old man remembered the many pleasant mornings he spent back home. The radio was playing in the background discussing this weekend's town's county fair.

Then the phone rang and it was Zachary. He wanted Xuan to accompany him to a local barbecue restaurant. Xuan told himself he would finish Zach off today once and for all.

"Hello?"

"Hey, bud. It's me, Zach." Xuan closed his eyes, trying not to curse.

"What happened now?"

"Joshua will help me."

"You told him about the loan shark?"

"Yeah. He's willing to help me out."

"Do you want to bring him into this?"

Zachary paused, considering saying something else.

"Look, let's talk about it at the restaurant."

"Ok."

"The Pit Room at noon. See you there, bud."

It was almost noon and Xuan got dressed. The old man grew tired, thinking about killing Zachary. This wasn't for a man his age. Xuan gathered some poisonous herbs and made a clear liquid. Xuan would poison Zach if he couldn't kill him with his knife.

The restaurant was nearby and the sun was blazing. Since the restaurant had reservations, Xuan waited until he was called. The place was packed for lunch.

"Hello, do you have a reservation, sir?" asked a gentleman.

Xuan panicked, afraid of holding up the line. "It should be under the name of Zachary Hamilton." The young man searched through a few pages of the reservation book while Xuan tapped his foot. "Here we go." Xuan was then invited inside and directed to Table 20. The restaurant's inside resembled a maze with the partitions separating the customers. Xuan followed the waiter and Zachary saw Xuan approaching. He stood up and embraced the old man.

"We've been waiting awhile for you." Zachary patted Xuan and led him inside to the table. They had already ordered and their plates was nearly empty. "Don't mind us. We were dead hungry and didn't know how late you'd be," said Zach, scratching the back of his head.

"Long time no see," said Joshua smiling while shaking Xuan's hand.

"I know. Where have you been all of this time, Joshua?"

"I went to Oklahoma on a business trip. It took longer than expected. I'm happy to be back. Too damn hot down there."

"I hear it's beautiful, though."

"Oklahomans live simple. It felt like I was living in England with the fucking Queen," laughed Joshua. "It was strange, the fucking women treat you like a king homesteading and shit. Big ass breasts and fucking rompers."

"We need to go," said Zachary.

A waiter came to the table, asking Xuan for his order. "A steak, rice and salad. And please bring me some red wine." The waiter jotted the order and asked, "How would you like your steak, sir?"

"Medium rare."

"That's a fucking pussy steak. You got to eat it rare, bud," said Joshua causing Zachary and the waiter to laugh.

"You're funny. But please give a steak - medium rare. Thank you."

The waiter nodded, leaving the area.

"I heard Zachary told you about what happened. It's a shame. Although I didn't know Tim well, he treated me well."

"Tim was a good friend. We served in Nam together. Great buddy. God rest his soul."

"Well, Joshua's in town to help an old buddy out, right?"

"Of course, I'll help as long as my friend here grants me a partnership in his company, I'll be glad to do so."

"So, you're setting stipulations?" asked Xuan.

"It's not quite a condition. My cash isn't even close to Tim's. There is no reason why I can't help an old friend." Joshua avoided looking at Xuan while eating.

"You'd take half of a poor man's assets, isn't that much to your advantage?"

Zachary stayed silent.

"Do you accept my offer, Zachary? Enough of this silly talk. This old man knows nothing."

Zachary stared at Xuan. "He's a long-time friend who only wants to help me, Xuan. Don't be so damn serious. We've been buddies since the old days back in Nam." Zachary winked at Joshua and Xuan just shook his head.

The waiter set Xuan's food down as the old man never experienced such luxury. As he ate, his mind shifted to executing his plan.

"When Joshua lends me the money, I can get rid of the loan shark once and for all."

"You shouldn't have gone to him in the first place. You are playing with your life."

"We had no choice, Xuan, and I didn't call you here to argue. We are grown-ups."

Xuan enjoyed the food, promising himself that he'd come here to eat again.

Then, the old man changed plans over his next target; making it Joshua. It wasn't the right time for

Zach, so after eating, Xuan suddenly got up. "I'll be leaving, gentleman."

"So soon. It was a pleasure meeting you Xuan. Maybe, we'll see each other again," said Joshua, not looking.

"I'll be in touch, Zach."

Zachary shook hands, and Xuan left, not shaking Joshua's.

Xuan was back home doing laundry as his clothes had piled up for days. He mopped the basement floor and went upstairs, pulling out his favorite book "The Art of War" from the bookshelf. Xuan had read it many times, but every time he did, it felt like the first time. After reading a few chapters, the old man fell asleep with the book in his hands.

Xuan Lang had the same dream night after night; reminiscences of his daughter and wife with him at the beach, laughing. Binh was practicing swimming with her father while the ocean's waves vibrated. His wife, Phuong was preparing sandwiches underneath a rainbow umbrella. It was a classic moment Xuan will never forget.

An hour later, the old man awoke, sweating. The dream always ended with him losing them. Xuan's wailings echoed throughout the house. This pain left a lasting hole in his heart. He got out of bed, splashing water on his face but couldn't wash away the thoughts. He went downstairs and took some herbs from the cupboard. The suspense was becoming worse than the day of his family's funeral.

Ethan was alone working for the last few days, so Xuan went by to check on him. Before going, he made the young man a sandwich.

"I've been worried about you." Ethan pulled out a chair for Xuan.

"I've been very busy for the last few days. Hopefully, I can make it up." Xuan pulled out the sandwich and Ethan's eyes lit up.

"How are things going?"

"Not well, only a few customers came." As Ethan ate, the scene reminded Xuan of his daughter craving for a snack in the middle of the night.

"As you were. I'll be in the storage room checking inventory." He went over the logs from the last few days and everything matched up. Ethan was a very responsible young adult.

A customer came in causing Xuan to halt. He overheard Ethan interacting with the customer.

"Hello, sir. How may I help you?"

"Do you have chamomile?"

Xuan heard a bit of shuffling. "Yes, we do. Just a moment, please."

"Here you are," said Ethan wrapping the herbs neatly. "That will be two dollars, sir."

Xuan thought about leaving him the store once his mission was accomplished.

"Sir, it's almost eight. Should we close for the evening?"

Ethan caught Xuan reading the newspaper, not paying attention. "Oh, sure Ethan, you can go. I'll close. Thank you. You've done great."

"You look tired. I'm here to help, you know."

"Your mother will worry. We don't want her to, do we?"

"Okay, I'll be in first thing in the morning." Ethan walked out and Xuan followed him.

"Take the day off. It's Sunday. I don't think we'll have a lot of customers."

It was nightfall and the streets were empty. At his doorsteps, the old man saw his right window open. Xuan knew something was wrong because he never opened them ever. He opened the door quietly, taking his pistol from the flowerpot. There was a loud crash upstairs and Xuan knew someone was inside.

Xuan crept up the stairs. His heart was racing more when approached his bedroom door sighting a man in a suit. It was Zachary rummaging through his drawers and Xuan couldn't believe what he was witnessing.

"What are you doing here?" Xuan spoke, holding his Baretta. Zachary stopped, getting up slowly.

"I can explain, Xuan it's not what you imagine."

"You killed them!"

"Killed who?"

"My wife and daughter."

"Listen, Xuan, I can explain." Xuan didn't have time for excuses. He aimed at Zachary's head.

"What did you say to my wife while you were raping her?"

Zachary backed up with his hands up. "I, I—".

"You have brought them hell in this life. Now, I'll make you a hundred times more."

Xuan twisted the silencer on the nuzzle but it wasn't the right size. Zachary's sweat was pouring down his face and Xuan was enjoying every second of his despair.

"Please don't kill me Xuan, I can help you."

"Do you think I'm here on vacation?" Xuan spat in Zach's face. "I've been following all of you for years; pursuing every last one of your feeble steps." Xuan pressed the pistol to Zach's forehead, causing him to wince.

"Why are you here inside my house, you fucking bastard?"

"Joshua wanted to know more about you. Please, I didn't want to. If you let me go, I promise you'll never see me again."

Xuan stared at how pathetic Zachary seemed.

"By the way, say hi to Tim, will you? I'm sure you'll spend some time together in hell." Xuan shot Tim in the forehead, watching his body hit the ground. As much as it appeared psychotic, the old man enjoyed it. Xuan then dragged the body to the basement. He was mopping up the blood when someone had knocked.

"I'm coming!" shouted Xuan as he closed the basement door. His shirt covered in blood and he yanked it off. The knocks became noisier.

"Just a minute!" He examined to see if any blood was left. Then, the old man opened the door observing Katherine, Ethan, and another next-door-neighbor.

"We heard a gunshot from your house! Are you okay?" said Katherine.

"Oh! Yeah, I was cleaning out my gun, and it fired accidentally."

"Do you have a license, sir?" said the woman behind Ethan and Katherine, scrunching.

"I do. I'm not a criminal, ma'am. Ask my associates, Katherine and Ethan."

"Yeah, he's good, Maribel."

"I hope you're okay. I'd be scared to death. You could have killed yourself," said Katherine.

"I'm sorry to disturb you. I'll let an expert do my gun cleaning from now on."

"Ok, Xuan. Have a good night."

Katherine, Ethan, and Maribel left and Xuan closed the door, returning to his bedroom. The blood on the carpet wasn't easy to clean up. It took almost two hours of scrubbing to remove the stains.

Xuan had to get Zach's body out of the house. He decided to dump it at a nearby hill during the night. He cut up Zachary's body and bagged up the body parts. Quietly, the old man waited for the right time to dispose of the remains.

ZACHARY'S funeral procession was dull and Xuan was forced to go in order to conceal his motive. During the sea of continuous tears and hymns, Xuan felt light-headed. He tried to avoid meeting with Zach's family members.

Xuan dumped Zach's body in the river instead of the hill because of dogs barking. Two days following, the body was found and there are still no suspects. As Xuan stood alongside Joshua Warren and Matthew Jones, Matthew kept chatting and didn't seem saddened by the news.

"Zachary was a great man. It's a shame he had to go like this," said Matthew.

"God takes the best from us. Rest in peace, bud," added Joshua bowing.

Xuan breathed as Zachary's wife approached.

"Will you be joining us for dinner?" she asked, teary-eyed.

"I'll be there." Xuan smiled, weakly. Zachary's two sons were alongside her, holding her tightly. Ben, Ronald, and Duong were having a chat with some of Zachary's old friends from the Marines and Xuan walked over.

"Gentlemen."

"Xuan Lang, it's been a while," said Duong, raising his drink.

"Drinking at a funeral? Talk about class," reflected Xuan. "It's unfortunate seeing one another on such circumstances."

Xuan perceived Ben, Ronald and Duong weren't close to Zachary, inferring from their unfriendly expressions.

"It's such a tragedy; no one deserves such a horrific end. Nobody deserves to die, period," said Duong.

"He was a kind-hearted man even when people cheating him," said Ben.

"It's a shame," replied Xuan.

"The man was up the ass in debt. I heard he was partners with Tim in the fishing business," said Ronald.

"Such gossip," said Xuan, looking at Joshua. They knew the truth.

They left to the reception to get food and offer

their condolences. Zachary's sons came over to the table asking if they needed something. The men waved "no" and proceeded on chatting. Xuan saw they were talking business and wasn't interested. The old man then excused himself.

Meanwhile, Joshua Warren walked towards the bar and Xuan sat next to him.

"What are we drinking today?"

"You wanted this to happen, didn't you?"

"What do you mean?"

"How was Zach murdered after telling you everything?"

Xuan ignored, requesting a drink.

"I'll find out everything on you, Xuan Lang. There's some fishy about you being here."

That was the wrong thing to say. "Shall I also expose you and your army friends for the horrific murders and rapes in Vietnam?"

Joshua was bewildered. His face became blue knowing the old man kenned their darkest secret.

"I know everything, you fucking bastard. And after your drink, I'd advise you to get out of here before everyone here knows." Xuan smiled as the waiter came.

"Hurry up; your clock is ticking," chuckled Xuan, getting up after finishing his drink. Joshua got up quickly and walked.

"What are you going to do?" questioned Joshua

when they reached the parking lot; feet away from Joshua's vehicle.

"I think you and I know what's next." Xuan pulled out his Baretta and pointed signalling Joshua to get inside. Joshua started the engine, driving off.

"It's such a shame we won't have a chance to say goodbye to Miranda." She was Joshua's wife, and because of her addiction, she was told to stay home.

"My friends will see I'm missing and will fucking kill you. You fucking Chink bastard."

"Shut the fuck up and drive. Don't stop until we reach the Fred Hartman Bridge. It's a nice day for swimming, huh!"

Joshua tried slowing down. "Keep driving and don't even think about doing anything stupid. I know where your family lives," said Xuan pressing the barrel to the side of Joshua's head.

"You didn't think this through. Did you?"

Xuan chuckled. When they reached the bottom of the bridge, Xuan told Joshua to get out and turn off the engine. Xuan instructed Joshua to get on the pavement. "You'll fucking pay for this, you fucking chink bastard."

"Never once will I feel regret." Xuan spat in Joshua's face. "Climb over and I will not repeat."

Joshua looked around, trying to signal for anyone to help. It was dark and the cars kept going across.

"Nobody will help you, Josh. This is it."

Joshua climbed over the rail onto the bridge's platform. The view below was horrifying; large rocks and a flowing river.

"Your buddies are waiting for you in hell. Have fun." Xuan poked Joshua in the back with the gun and told him "Jump."

With one look, Joshua jumped to his death. Xuan gazed at his body while it crashed on the rocks into the water.

Xuan didn't return home. He decided it was time to head to Ben's house in Joshua's car minutes away. Ben came home right after the funeral and his wife and children were out front barbecuing. Xuan loosened his tie and walked through the family's front garden.

"Xuan?" said Ben squinting. Ben's wife escorted their children inside with their aunt.

"Hello, Ben. I'm sorry to interrupt, but our friend, Joshua is missing. I don't know where. He mentioned a lake."

"Oh, my! What happened?" His wife cut in.

"Joshua felt drained after the funeral and was driving me home. He stopped and when I went to pee, I came back and he wasn't there."

"We need to call the police right away," said Ben lowering the spatula after turning over burgers.

"I think he may be out there roaming around."

Ben's wife ran to call the police but had no idea how to describe. She told her sister to watch the kids while she, Ben and Xuan go out to find Joshua. Ben and his wife jumped in Joshua's car with Xuan in the passenger seat. They kept driving to the wrong areas, and after hours of searching, they stopped on the roadside.

"Why would Joshua leave you? This is kind of strange." Ben and his wife kept asking.

"Before I left the car, he was saying he was tired of life. I thought he was joking."

They drove off again and minutes later, reached a lake that Xuan said resembled the place they stopped at. They searched with their flashlights, calling his name and he was nowhere to be found.

On the way back, the couple told Xuan their life story; how and where they first met and when they bought their first home and had children. Xuan wasn't interested, just making small talk here and there. Ben told Xuan to come inside for coffee in the couple's living room.

"Bethany and Lucas are lovely kids, but I think we'll let their tutors go because we can't afford them any longer. Tutors are getting more expensive." Xuan listened to Andrea's non-stop chattering and wanted to fall asleep. They waited hoping to receive good news about Joshua while Xuan only wanted to kill Ben but couldn't.

"They won't need a tutor. You'll see they'll be top of their classes. Just keep them focused," said Xuan. Any minute, the police would be on their way. Sadly, the old man had to stick around.

"Let's hope so." She took a long sip, and then Ben joined them. "These sheriffs are taking long. It's almost midnight," said Joshua after talking with the police for the third time in hours. Ben lived in a rural town outside of Houston and the police said they were on their way.

"What are you over there talking about?" Joshua sat down next to Andrea, holding her hand.

"Bethany and Lucas, of course, honey."

"Those little rascals." Ben and Andrea laughed while Xuan smiled. He gave them privacy; turning away when they kissed.

Forty-five minutes passed and Xuan said, "I think I'll be heading home soon. I live rather far from here. The police are taking us serious, so I'll leave you my number just in case." As Xuan was getting up, the sheriff's car lights flashed outside.

Xuan, Ben, and Andrea walked out on the porch, greeting them.

"Good evening," said a fat sheriff. He tipped his hat and proceeded to say, "I'm sorry, but your friend, Joshua Warren appears to have taken his life."

The couple and Xuan gasped.

"What!?" replied Ben.

"Where?" asked Xuan.

"Down the Old Lakewood Pond next to the Fred Hartman Bridge. It's not deep, but the cliffs below it are deadly. It appears he jumped. We have some questions for you since you were the last one to see him."

"No problem, officer. I'm willing to help."

"Why would he do this? He was such a happy man." Andrea clung onto Ben and didn't want to let go.

The sheriffs interviewed Xuan and then told him it was all they needed.

As they were leaving, they offered their deepest sympathies.

"VIETNAM WAR HERO, JOSHUA WARREN COMMITS SUICIDE"

THE OLD MAN laughed as he read the front headline. His smile disappeared when he read through the article and spotted, *"Case is still under investigation for potential witnesses."*

"What witnesses?" yelled Xuan tossing the paper. "What does a man in grief have to do to get some recognition?"

Xuan knew he had to move on. The last time he saw Ben was the night of Joshua's disappearance a week ago, and it was time to kill him. No one knew of these men's past wrongs and Xuan hated that they were seen as hometown heroes. He vowed to expose them for what they have done even if it meant taking his own life.

Xuan was eating, thinking about how to proceed with Ben. It had to be quick. When he was nearly finished eating, someone gently knocked.

The old man was confused, placing his dishes in the sink. He then opened the door and it was Anna, Tim's widow.

"What are you doing here?" He looked around, afraid if anyone had seen her come.

"I read about your other victim, Zachary Hamilton. How clever you are!" She brushed past and walked inside. Not wasting time, she got comfortable, plopping next to his food.

"Who's next?" Anna grabbed the newspaper and read the headline — VIETNAM WAR HERO, JOSHUA WARREN COMMITS SUICIDE—. Xuan shushed her and yanked it from her, setting it on the countertop.

"Isn't that a lie?" snickered Anna.

"You have no business here."

"You're wrong about that, Mr. Killer. I do because you killed my fucking husband." Anna took out red lipstick from her handbag.

"What do you want from me?"

Anna took her time answering, putting it on while staring in her pocket mirror.

"Ten grand." She closed the mirror, waiting for the old man's response.

"You're fucking crazy. You have to go." He picked up Anna's handbag and pushed her towards the door.

"How nice of you to send me directly to the police station. Isn't it?"

Xuan moved in front of her. "You wouldn't dare."

"If you give me ten grand, I won't. I know you have money. All you fucking Chinks do." Anna tapped her foot, indicating she didn't have much time. "Give me the money and you can have Tim's cabin in Austin. I'm leaving town and don't need it."

Xuan looked at her, disgusted he was being bribed. He went upstairs to his safe and placed the money in a paper bag. When he came back down, he tossed the bag to Anna.

"It's all there. You can count it at home, but it's time for you to go. I have work to do." Xuan opened the door, not giving Anna satisfaction.

"As you were. Have a nice life, Xuan and remember what goes around, comes around." Anna handing Xuan the keys to the cabin and left.

Xuan picked up Ben's number off the kitchen counter. He needed a plot to get him over. He told Ben he wanted to rehabilitate a cabin given to him. Since Ben renovated homes, the old man told him the money would be good if he can help.

Ben Rogers came alone. Little did he know, he was taking a trip to his grave. Xuan got his gear ready and left extra fuel in his car. His plan was for them to stay at the cabin for the day and at night, he'd make his move and burn the place down.

Xuan hadn't heard from Katherine or Ethan in days. When he was about to stop by the shop, Ben pulled up to the front of the house, beeping his horn. "Xuan!"

"Coming!" Xuan grabbed his duffle bag and left.

"Let's go fix em' up, bud!"

Ben drove for two hours in the woods to Tim's cabin. When they were driving, Xuan told Ben to look around. The beauty of wilderness struck Ben. It was relaxing and for at least a day, he'd be away from the constant noise of his two children.

"We're here," said Xuan when they arrived. They went inside, leaving their things on the porch.

"It's nice. We can do lots of things at this place. I can already see." snickered Ben, roaming around the cabin.

Xuan was left to carry the burden of this place for one day. Xuan only needed it for one reason; to get rid of Ben Rogers.

"I bought it when I first got to Texas. Do you like

it?" Xuan cleaned off the table and unpacked the food he prepared.

"Who wouldn't like a place like this? It's so peaceful." Ben looked out of the window, captivated by the stunning landscape. Xuan opened two cans of cola while Ben wasn't looking and put a sleeping pill in one.

"You're right. Too bad! I don't have time to come out here more often. The fresh air could do me some good," said Xuan while taking a bite out from his sandwich. Ben sat down nearby, unwrapping his.

"This place is perfect for a picnic, and we are stuck with these--"

"Better something than nothing." Xuan gave Ben a can of cola.

"So, where shall we start?" asked Xuan.

"The front. As you can see, there are a few holes on the sides and the wind blows in at night."

"Next, change the boards. Maybe with oak with a touch of enamel. It would look amazing."

Xuan wasn't paying attention.

"The last thing is the kitchen. To be honest with you, Xuan, it looks like a shithole. If Andrea was here, she'd give it a good makeover."

"Give me a list of the things you need and I'll buy them."

"Will do. Plus, we'll be done in no time fixing this place up," Ben reassured. They went on talking about

Tim, Zachary and Joshua and Xuan was getting restless, waiting for Ben to fall asleep.

After an hour, Ben started dozing off. Xuan waited a little longer before going to get the gas tank. "Ben?" The old man shook him to see if he was still conscious. "Ben?" The man was knocked out cold. Xuan got the tank out of the trunk and splashed it around the cabin. "Damn, I forgot the lighter." Xuan hurried back and found it in the glove department. Before burning the cabin, Xuan relived the moments he saw Ben, laughing with the others. He dropped the lighter, causing the cabin burst into flames. The old man watched as the cabin burned and its smoke was increasing. The old man pulled off, gratified that Ben Rodgers was on his way to Hell.

———

Ben's wife, Andrea was in shock by the unexpected death of her husband. She came to Xuan's house three days after the funeral.

"What will I do alone with these kids? They're broken by the loss of their father." Andrea cried constantly, sitting at Xuan's dining room table.

"You need to stay strong. Ben was an excellent man." Xuan placed a cup of tea in front of her.

"He should have asked you to come along. I don't know what he was doing out there alone."

"Zach had a cabin that Ben wanted to renovate, I heard. I wasn't feeling well, so I left him earlier. Ben said he had work to do out there."

"Terrible," grumbled Andrea as she cried not wanting to go away. The kids were at a neighbor's house. After Xuan had told her that the kids needed her at this very moment, Andrea finally decided to leave.

Xuan pulled out the files of his targets. Now that Tim, Zachary, Joshua, and Ben were all gone, it was time to focus on Matthew, Ronald, and for last, Duong Gian.

Xuan recognized his shop needed his keeping. On the way there, he stopped at a park to clear his mind. The old man felt so mentally fatigued. Xuan looked at the families, spending time with one another. It was a sight he dearly missed.

The old man left and saw Katherine and Ethan inside the shop from out front. It was odd seeing her there, helping Ethan. Xuan greeted them and they looked up surprised.

"Long time no see, Xuan. Where have you been?" Katherine came over, embracing him.

"Here and there, visiting colleagues who recently

passed," Katherine let go allowing Ethan to shake the old man's hand.

"We heard about the awful news."

"You must be feeling miserable. I'm so sorry." Ethan offered Xuan his seat.

"These were good buddies. It's sad to see them go."

"In better news, it's been a pleasure operating the store," continued Katherine.

"Our lives have been better since you moved here and offered me this job," said Ethan. "I get a chance to spend time with my mother and save money. Maybe I'll buy a Macintosh?"

"I'm glad to hear that young man. Even when I'm not here one day, you must help out your mother?"

Katherine and Ethan looked at each other. "Wait, does this mean you're leaving, Xuan?"

Xuan lowered his head. "No, not yet but one day."

Their stares made him feel awkward. Xuan couldn't reveal anything. If he did, he would have to kill them.

"Xuan, are you listening?" Katherine waved her hand.

"Sorry. What were you saying?"

"Where will you go?"

"Back to Vietnam. America is a beautiful but home is home."

"I'm sure your family misses you," said Ethan.

Xuan wasn't close to his relatives and grew distant after the shocking death of his two angels. "I'm sure they do."

As they were talking, Xuan hadn't noticed three men in front of the shop, looking around. They finally walked inside and Xuan stood up, surprised. It was Matthew, Ronald, and Duong.

"What are you fellows doing here?" said Xuan shaking their hands.

"Hello, Xuan. We have a few questions if it isn't too much trouble," said Duong looking at Ethan and Katherine who got his drift.

"Will you be okay, Xuan?" asked Katherine.

"It's fine. These gentlemen are close buddies. Give us a few minutes, please. Thank you."

Ethan and Katherine went to the back and Xuan turned his attention to them.

"To what do I owe the pleasure, gentleman?"

"We need some answers," added Matthew.

"Please, sit." Xuan pointed with only Duong sitting, keeping his eyes on Xuan.

"We don't want to waste time. You've been close to us and it seems to be a coincidence that our friends have died since you came," said Duong.

Xuan knew they had nothing. "It's strange, I agree. I even think someone is following me. That's why I have two workers at all times here. Who knows, maybe I'm next?"

"Do you have enemies here in America?" asked Matthew.

"Yes, a lot." thought Xuan. "None I know of."

"I moved here from the Philippines around two years ago and never had an argument. Why would someone want to kill an old guy like me? I'm someone's grandfather," joked Xuan causing the men to laugh.

"I don't know. Someone is out to kill us. It seems like every fucking week," expressed Ronald.

"You should stick together more often."

"You mean we should stick together." Matthew corrected Xuan.

"You need protection, Xuan. You're more helpless here than we are," replied Duong.

"Listen, I am grateful for your suggestions but I don't want to get caught up in this. Maybe we can talk about this another time."

"You don't want to hear about it. Well, me too. Fuck it. Let's celebrate life tonight," said Ronald.

To life then!" said Matthew clearing his throat while crossing his arms.

"We'll be having dinner. Every month, we have these dinner gatherings and tonight you're invited".

"Ok, just write down the address."

As Matthew was writing, Xuan pondered which of the men would be his next victim. Not Duong, the Vietnamese traitor would save him for last. He portrayed himself as the leader and deserved a heinous ending.

Matthew was full of himself but was the most honest out the bunch.

Ronald was arrogant, flaunting his wealth to no end. No one wouldn't miss him if he was taken out.

The three men left and Xuan noticed Katherine and Ethan also had left. They deserved some time off and Xuan called, telling them he had an important dinner to go to and to take the rest of the day off.

Xuan closed the shop and went home to pick out his best suit for the occasion.

"THIS WAY, SIR." A waitress led Xuan through the crowded restaurant packed with rich kids and parents. Xuan assumed Duong chose it because of its white-bread atmosphere.

"Thank you." Xuan reached where Matthew, Ronald, and Duong were seated.

"Glad you could make it, Xuan." smiled Matthew, telling the old man to sit.

"This place is packed, isn't it?"

"This has become our favorite restaurant. It's one of Houston's most celebrated among the youngsters as you can see," added Duong, calling over a waiter.

Xuan looked around, seeing what appeared to be horseplay. "Did you guys order already?"

"No, we waited for you this time," said Ronald.

"So Xuan, tell us about that cabin in the woods," started Duong.

Xuan took his time, answering. "Honestly, Tim was going to sell it to me, but we couldn't close the deal."

"Such a shame it burned to pieces." Duong looked at Xuan as if he knew something.

"If Tim was kind enough to sell it to you, he must have trusted you'd do good with it. He always told me it wasn't for sale," added Matthew.

"Wow, really? Anna had dreams of designing that old thing. By the way, where is she anyway?"

"Maybe she's fucking that young carpenter, Billy? That woman has always been a whore."

Everyone chuckled.

"I never met her, so I wouldn't know," continued Xuan.

The waiter put their food down and filled their glasses with beer.

"Do you have something to say Ronald?" asked Xuan disappointed with all the questioning. "Just keep playing the victim," conceived Xuan.

"Not at all, just curious how the cabin burned down by a simple fire. Ben doesn't doze off too long."

"I don't know," said Xuan.

"Then, it has to be Anna. No one else knew besides her where the cabin was. But you were there before, right?"

"I don't remember exactly. Tim took me to a lot of places. Why are you insinuating I did something, Ronald?"

"Maybe it was an accident as they said," added Duong.

"Sorry, Xuan. I'm only looking at the situation, that's all. Don't take things personal."

Ronald couldn't stop staring at Xuan and Xuan noticed. He wasn't to take out all three at once and the old man couldn't let Ronald take the strings into his own hands even if it meant killing him tonight. Xuan's eyes slowly drifted to Ronald who was chewing like it was his last meal. Xuan deemed it such. Matthew and Duong were chatting while Xuan was planning his move on Ronald. It had to be done quickly, meaning right here, right now.

After a few beers, the guys chatted about business. Xuan brought a bottle of poisonous herbs made into liquid form, and it was his most deadly weapon. He ordered a bottle of champagne and Ronald finished his first glass in one swallow.

"We're going out for a smoke. We'll be back." Xuan felt like the Lord was on his side by sending Matthew and Duong away. Ronald was a heavy drinker but didn't smoke. Xuan offered him another glass as Ronald's eyes bobbed on a tall blonde with big breasts passing by. This was the perfect chance to get him.

"Go get her, Ron. She's looking at you. Look at those damn tits," said Xuan hyping Ron up.

"You don't have to say anything. I'm already getting up."

Xuan looked at how stupid this guy was. While Ronald was chatting, Xuan pulled out the liquid poison and dropped it all in Ronald's glass. Meantime, the blonde turned down Ronald, and he came back embarrassed. He blasted her while sipping on his drink.

Xuan observed Ronald and then excused himself. He waited next to the bar, watching him. For two minutes, Ronald was choking and then became unconsciousness, falling to the ground. A waiter yelled for help and the people in the restaurant started screaming. Duong and Matthew ran back inside as Xuan tried giving Ronald CPR. Ronald Ravens was dead.

Within minutes, the medics came to take the body out, and the police interviewed everyone. They then courted off the restaurant which was ordered to close.

"How did this happen? He was okay when we left." Matthew's quivering was the only thing heard in the empty restaurant.

"You should go back home, I'll talk with the police," insisted Xuan. Ronald and Matthew left while Xuan didn't wait around much longer. He grabbed a bottle of wine and rejoiced once he arrived home.

· · ·

"Five down and two more to go," the old man thought as he pondered over the last victim. I could have killed all of them, but it would have made him look suspicious being the only person alive from the group. For the rest of the evening, Xuan cooked dinner enjoying a bowl of Pho. After finishing, he went to the basement and grabbed up a box.

There were many pictures of his family; all happy moments they spent together. He cherished the day he returned from the army and it was his birthday. Binh and Phoung made his favorite cake, along with some tasty Banh mì. Their smiles were priceless and he remembered them for ages.

Xuan then imagined about his return home. He'd be the only one alive. He shoved the pictures back in the box and kicked it under the kitchen table. Xuan's patience was running out but he knew it would be all over soon.

The following morning, Xuan got out of bed thinking about his next target, Matthew Jones. But there was one problem, he didn't have his address or phone number.

When he reached the kitchen, he heard the news-paper hitting the door. Xuan brought it inside, concentrating on the front page headline -- POSSIBLE SERIAL KILLER IN HOUSTON'S SUBURBS --. The old mand didn't see himself as such; he was only seeking revenge. If Xuan was in the army like his victims, the Americans would have given him a purple heart for killing the Gooks as they labeled them.

He set the paper down. "Damn reporters have nothing else to talk about." His whisper was loud enough to hear as he went to go shower.

"These old bones are kicking in," said Xuan as he put on his robe. He loved the mornings in Texas especially before people went to work. The old man looked out the window and saw Katherine and Ethan walking down the street with groceries. The young man's hand had a wrap on it and Katherine was struggling, carrying most of the bags. Xuan ran outside to help.

"Hand them to me," commanded Xuan as he approached. They were surprised to see the old man in his robe again.

"Xuan?"

"You should come over for breakfast. Mom's cooking bacon and eggs," said Ethan.

Xuan looked at Ethan's hand. "What happened, young man?"

"I was riding my bike and didn't notice the tire was flat. I fell off when I braked."

Xuan slightly grinned, praying they didn't hear

about Ronald Raven's death. The borough was small enough that everyone knew even if a tire was stolen.

"You went shopping injured," joked Xuan.

"It's Mom's fault. We could have taken two trips or a taxi home," complained Ethan.

"Don't baby him; he isn't handicapped. That cut is smaller than a pinhole," remarked Katherine as they reached their steps.

"Let's go inside. I'll start breakfast."

Xuan's mind traveled back to happier times back home. "How could I say no to bacon and eggs?"

Xuan helped her set the groceries down and sat next to Ethan. Just like the time when they first met officially. "So, Xuan. Did you decide on when you're leaving town yet?" asked Ethan.

"Yes, maybe soon. My house in Vietnam is now fixed up. A typhoon struck it a few months ago."

"Wow, I imagine it's beautiful in Vietnam. I've read many stories on the war and even saw Apocalypse Now."

"Ethan!" yelled Katherine.

"Ok, mom. Sorry!"

"My house has three rooms, a large kitchen like your mother's, and one big front room. It's not much, but we manage."

"You can start setting the table for your mother, Ethan," yelled Katherine from the kitchen.

Ethan began standing up but Xuan stopped him, putting his finger to his mouth. "Sit. I'll do it. Tell me where everything is."

Ethan pointed to the cupboard on the left and Xuan helped Ethan set the table before Katherine came in with the food. The three had a long chat about Ethan's living on campus. The young man got a four-year scholarship and Xuan was proud of him. The old man was glad they didn't mention the recent murders in the town.

Xuan excused him, recognizing he started caring about Ethan and his mother too much. This wasn't the old man's plan. When he unlocked his door, Matthew was inside sitting, looking at TV.

"Matthew?" Xuan gasped setting down the food Katherine had given him. "Hello, Xuan. I didn't mean to trespass but Duong's working today and I'm buying a new car. You're the only one I trust being around these days."

"How did you get in?"

"I knocked and turned the knob finding it unlocked. I hope you don't mind. We're buds, right?" Matthew scratched his head as he explained. "No problem. I wished you would have called first. You don't know whom I might have had in here." "Sorry, bud but are you up for a little drive?" said Matthew walking to the kitchen and pulling out a juice carton from the fridge.

"Sure, let me get dressed." Xuan looked at the box of photos under the table. He pretended to straighten things up, throwing a rag over it.

"I'll be right here."

There's was no time to waste as the perfect chance came to kill Matthew. The old man devised a plan as he got dressed. "It must be my lucky day."

Xuan and Matthew rode for thirty minutes to the Helfman Ford dealership. As they drove through the hot sun, Matthew blasted country music and Xuan tried blocking out the sound. When he spoke, Matthew lowered the volume.

"I like this car, to be honest. How much did it cost you?" asked Xuan, looking out the window.

"Not much." Matthew made a U-turn. "What do you want to get now?"

"Maybe a Ford Pinto."

Matthew nodded and Xuan was thinking about his plan. If they went out for a test drive, he could poison him; causing the car to drive off a cliff. Xuan smiled imaging as they pulled up in the car lot.

Matthew talked with a salesman while Xuan walked around checking out the cars. Some were so expensive that he believed no one would ever buy them.

Matthew was fixated on buying the Ford Pinto, and the salesman offered him to go on a test drive. Xuan got in first and Matthew slowly drove off. Xuan just needed to get Mattew unconscious. "Damn, I left the beers back home. What to do?" realized the old man. He looked down seeing there was a fire extinguisher underneath.

Once they reached an isolated area, Xuan spoke. "Matthew, I think the back tire is losing air" The car came to a sudden halt, and Matthew turned to him.

"Are you fucking serious?"

Matthew jumped out and slammed the door. He walked to the back and inspected it.

"Is it this one?" He got on his knees, sharply observing it.

"Yeah, that one." Xuan unlocked the fire extinguisher and got out, seeing Matthew bent down.

"Are you sure it's this one, I don't see anything wrong with it?" Matthew was about to get up and Xuan hit him in the back of the head. Matthew laid on the ground stretched out but was still conscious.

Xuan dragged him and put him in the passenger seat. He drove away, stepping on the gas with full force. The old man drove until he reached a mountain range a few miles down the road. He pulled Matthew's body over to the driver's seat and strapped his seatbelt. Then, he got out and pushed it towards the end of a cliff with all his force. When it reached the edge, it got stuck but after pushing it harder; the car flipped over and fell to its end, causing a big explosion.

As Xuan walked down the road, he was lucky someone spotted him in an old pickup truck. "Are you okay mate?"

"I'm lost. My car broke down some miles down. The engine died."

The man tried chatting, but Xuan told him he didn't speak English well. The man told him he was from Alabama and here working in Houston. As they drove, the man cursed complaining about traffic.

"Thank you," said Xuan when he reached his shop. The man saluted him, saying they could hook up in the evenings at a bar a few miles away. Xuan knew he'd never see him again. Once home, he listened to a message from Duong on his answering machine. The old man knew time was ticking as he edged closer to ending his misery.

XUAN SPENT the next few days home. Duong left messages on Xuan's answering machine indicating he was on the verge of committing suicide. The police found Matthew's body charred so badly they couldn't do an autopsy. The dealership wanted payment for the car from Ronald's girlfriend and the news coverage on the ordeal was on every TV set in the town.

Xuan didn't see Katherine nor Ethan before they left for a family vacation. It was good they'd taken off because Xuan was close to ending his mission and they'd never see him again. Once, Katherine told Xuan about the murder of her first husband five years ago while he was on a business trip in Peru. Ethan was young and Katherine felt lonely until she met her current husband, whom she had a stepson but the man was always away working. That son stayed with the father's mother and only came by a few times a year. Katherine focused more on Ethan than her husband. Xuan was surprised she moved on so quickly and didn't seek revenge. He couldn't close his eyes at night in peace knowing his family's killers were still alive breathing.

Xuan thought deeply about his homeland during this time off. The food is impeccable and the best meals were on the streets - sitting on little plastic stools in the marketplaces. The food stands were open 24 hours and people of all ages would enjoy. Seafood was Xuan's favorite. He remembered a time when he would come close to the stove, while his wife Phoung was cooking and try to sneak a bite. She'd smack his hand and they'd laugh.

The phone rang and it snapped Xuan out of his daydream.

"Hello?"

"It's me, Duong."

Xuan cleared his throat. "Yes, I know."

"Why haven't you returned my calls. I'm fucking stressed."

"I've been busy with the shop. My workers have gone on vacation."

"Ok. I just wanted to let you know the neighborhood is having a veterans parade in about two hours. I hope you'll come and hear me speak."

"Sure, I'll be there. Where?"

"St. Greenwood. Everyone will be there. Don't worry! No one will try to kill us there."

"Then, I'll be there."

Xuan hung up and went to his bedroom picking out a suit. It was almost five and at six, the parade was beginning. He took a peek out the window and saw neighbors walking already towards the parade. Xuan would listen to his speech and execute his plan on Duong later in the evening. The old man was thankful Ethan and Katherine were out of town.

It was 6 o'clock and Xuan left for the Parade. He followed seeing families were cheering and waving flags at the soldiers and band members. Xuan hated them all except those who defended freedom. He had the highest respect for anyone in the military being a former soldier himself. Walking through the crowd, he felt out of place. The old man knew his retaliation wouldn't happen here; there were too many people around.

The troops stood, waiting for the orders of their general to salute. Everyone crowded the stage area till Duong Dian appeared; carrying his address.

Duong came out minutes later, opening his paper to speak.

"Ladies and Gentleman. Thank you for coming out this evening. In the past few months, I've lost so much as I did in Nam. I saw life in its purest form taken away, and as destiny proves repeatedly, it can be relentless at times."

Xuan scrunched.

"My fellow soldiers, soulmates, friends and most importantly, brothers who lost their lives in defending liberty."

The crowd clapped and Xuan wanted to leave.

"God blessed me, five years ago when we, the seven men from Houston, were on their way to Nam to serve this country gracefully." Duong paused, gathering himself.

"Within the last few weeks, I feel defeated. Unfairly crushed by life, but it doesn't mean I'll stop fighting to bring justice! To put the one responsible behind bars for the rest of their pathetic life. There is no doubt there is one man behind all of this and I shall find him. I promise you."

The crowd cheered as Xuan was shocked. "Was that his cue that he knows?"

Duong was leaving and the old man left, not interested in seeing the soldiers march. As he was walking away, a voice shouted, "Xuan!" He kept walking and Duong ran towards him.

"That was a nice speech. Little shorter than I expected, but it was satisfying."

"You thought it wouldn't be any good?" Why didn't you stay to watch the soldiers march?"

"You're younger than me, Duong. An old man like myself can't do too much activity. I'd invite you over for a drink, but you're busy campaigning," said Xuan.

"I'm free. I said what I needed. Honestly, I don't like watching these soldiers marching. It's ROTC stuff."

They laughed as Duong was choking.

"Easy, easy, my friend. I live five minutes away."

They chatted and Xuan came up with praises about Duong's speech. "I lured the rabbit into the trap, at last," conceived Xuan.

"This is beautiful," praised Duong when they reached his home. Xuan noticed Ethan and Katherine were back in town. What are they doing here? They were cleaning up. Xuan tried dodging them but Katherine saw Xuan.

"Xuan!"

Gasping, Xuan turned around. "Hey Katherine. You're back so early. I hope all is well" Katherine approached them in the garden.

"We actually went to visit my mother. We wanted

to surprise her." She glanced at Duong. "Care to introduce me to your friend?" Katherine extended her hand out.

"This is Duong Gian, a Vietnam Vet."

Duong replied, "Nice to meet you, Madame."

"Katherine, may I invite you inside for a drink with my friend," proposed Xuan.

"Oh no, thank you. My pie's in the oven. Go on ahead."

"Nice to meet you again, Madame."

"You, too."

They went inside the house and Duong mentioned how cozy the place was.

"This reminds me of a family I once knew?" Duong sat as Xuan went close the door.

"I bought when I first laid eyes on it," Xuan said, taking off his coat.

"I'll get us some drinks." Xuan left not planning on poisoning Duong. He wanted the coward to suffer. The Vietnamese never should cross one another and he did.

Xuan brought two beers and Duong was stretched out on the couch with his eyes half-closed.

"You're tired already?" Xuan chuckled, handing him a beer.

"It's been a long day, filled with rehearsals. I didn't know the event was going to be that big."

The men chatted for hours and the clock showed 9 PM. Xuan was ready to go ahead with Duong's execution.

"Excuse me. I'll be back. I have to go to the bathroom."

"Ok."

Xuan went to the bedroom first, looking back to make sure Duong wasn't looking. Underneath the bed, he pulled out a rope he bought from the farmer's market for the occasion. He held it behind his back and close the bedroom door. When Xuan reached the bottom of the steps, he saw Duong with a photo in his hand. He gazed closer and saw it was from the box under the table. The box's lid was cast on the floor.

Duong chuckled. "These two women ring a bell. Don't they?" He said flicking the picture.

"What are you doing with that?"

"You killed my friends, didn't you?"

There was a long silence before they saw a butcher knife on the kitchen counter. They ran towards it, knocking each other down and the knife fell from the shaking.

"You bastard? I will kill you!"

Duong tried going for it, but Xuan hit him in the

head with a frying pan and put the rope around his neck, dragging him backwards.

"I remember their last words. Their pleas for help, the cries. Oh! it sounded so good," Duong said as he struggled to get loose from the old man's grip.

"Your friends are rotting in hell and you will, too."

Duong was desperately gasping for air. He then elbowed Xuan in the stomach, causing the old man to release him. He raced to the knife but Xuan's pain didn't stop him. When Duong bent to grab it, Xuan kicked him into the cabinets. Duong's head slammed into the hardwood and Xuan kicked him with his old boots. Duong was alive but streams of blood were spewing from his mouth.

Holding him in a chokehold, Xuan grabbed the knife and slit his throat. "Burn in the pits of hell alongside your friends." Xuan then stabbed Duong three times. Feeling like it wasn't enough, he stabbed twenty more times; each blow saw blood gushing in all directions. Seeing Duong was gone, Xuan pushed Duong's body off of him and embraced the moment. The old man got up off the floor, someone knocked and then opened the door.

"I brought you some pie; Thought you'd like it." It was Katherine. "Oh, my god!" she yelled dropping the pie.

She looked at the knife in Xuan's hands, holding her mouth. The woman trembled not moving an inch.

"Xuan, what did you do!?"

Katherine then realized Xuan was probably the cold-blooded murderer the police was looking for.

"Please, Katherine. I can explain. This man was a rapist and killer." His bloody hands tried touching her, but she pulled back. Xuan knew she'd go to the police but he couldn't kill her.

"This coward raped and murdered my wife and daughter. I'm asking you not to say anything."

Katherine stared remembering she forgave the murderer of her husband but couldn't find the same sympathy for Xuan.

"You'll go to prison, killer! I don't believe you were around my son!" said Katherine, running out slamming the door shut.

"I'm so sorry, Katherine!"

Xuan rushed packing his suitcase after washing his bloody hands. The old man dashed out of the door, ignoring the pain in his stomach from the hit by Duong.

He put on a baseball cap and wandered through the night, knowing that his face was probably on the news already.

The nearest motel was one mile away, and Xuan knew he could only stay there for one night. People on the street passed by him and he looked down; his cap shielded his eyes.

When he found the place, there was a middle-aged woman waiting behind the reception desk. She lowered her glasses when Xuan came in.

"A room for one, please." Xuan looked behind to see if anyone was trailing him.

"ID and credit card, please."

Xuan handed her his passport and said he only had cash. The woman was popping chewing gum looking over the passport and then went to get the room keys. A few couples passed through the lobby causing Xuan to look away.

He remembered the box of photos he left behind. Nearly every memory will be defunct and lost forever. The receptionist came back. She handed Xuan the keys. "Have a lovely stay."

"Room 34." Xuan passed through the hallway and the room was at the very end. He had trouble unlocking it at first. When he opened the door, he found it full of dust.

"I see they didn't even bother cleaning it." Frustrated, Xuan set his suitcase on the floor and locked the door. He looked out the window. There was no one outside.

Xuan sat on the bed, defeated. His life was

destroyed. He made one mistake of not locking the front door.

For two hours, he couldn't fall asleep weeping about what will happen now. Xuan believed his daughter and wife were disappointed since he got caught by Katherine.

"5 AM" showed the clock. The old man turned on the television and saw his image all plastered on the news with the headlines reading underneath: SERIAL KILLER IDENTIFIED - XUAN LANG FROM VIETNAM - MANHUNT UNDERWAY. "Goddamit, Katherine," yelled Xuan as he watched. Law enforcement agencies from all over Texas were searching everywhere. They showed images of Xuan's passport photo and the ones with his family from the box. The words, "WANTED" was written underneath his. Neighbors who never spoke to Xuan now were on camera uttering their suspicions.

Xuan Lang regretted not killing Katherine. If it wasn't for his decency unlike his enemy, he would have done so. It was a problem that will haunt him for the hours to come.

Minutes later, as Xuan was closing his eyes, steps could be heard thundering outside the door. He knew what it meant. The old man got up off the bed and walked over to the corner where he placed his suitcase.

"Xuan Lang! Responsible for the deaths of seven US Marines. This is the FBI. Come out and put your hands on the back of your head where we can see them." Police lights were flashing outside and dozens of deputies were taking up positions in every direction. Xuan pondered being locked up for the rest of his life or the likelihood of martyrdom. "My fate is in my hands," shouted Xuan.

He took out the Baretta and loaded it with one bullet. The FBI begged for him to surrender, but they didn't hear anything. "Breach the fucking door." When they did, Xuan Lang ended his life being the last one to murder.

DEBARE BALOGUN_

Lago's streets were crowded which was typical for the morning rush hour as people were on their way to work and school. Traffic on the road was stalled and Debare Balogun was running late for his morning meeting.

He hurried through the crowds with his shining silver suit. Pushing through the marketplaces, Debare was determined to get there on time as it was a twenty-minute walk to his shop.

Inside Balogun Jewellery, his secretary, Daraja Agu, stood behind the desk welcoming him. She wore a ponytail and was dressed modestly.

"Good day, sir."

"Morning, Daraja."

"The gentlemen are waiting for you."

"Thank you."

Debare walked faster. If the clients didn't accept his latest offer, it meant Balogun Jewellery wouldn't last much longer.

Debare's reputation wasn't the best in town. He was a scam artist and only few would work with him. Fixing his suit, he walked inside finding them seated at his roundtable.

"Morning, gentleman."

The men looked but didn't respond. Debare ignored them, setting down his suitcase.

"You're late."

"Traffic was bad."

"How's our project coming along?" asked Marcel, a Jew who was in Lagos trafficking diamonds and anything he could make money off of. He heard rumours of Debare's past business dealings but somehow, gave his support for this project.

"The gold transfer will begin in a few days, sir. We've made all the arrangements, so we just need your final deposit."

"We will not release the final deposit because our client has yet to receive the gold. Why is there a delay?"

"Uh, no sir, is there a problem?" Debare started sweating sensing he wasn't buying his story. Marcel whispered something to his partner in a suit beside him.

"The problem is you, Debare." Marcel picked up some papers he had on the table.

"Excuse me. Let me explain." Debare got up fixing his tie.

"You think you're fooling us, huh?" Marcel chuckled. "I know what you've been skimming money off the top. All the money; my men and I wasted on this damn project is in your bloody pockets." Marcel's fist banged on the table and its sound echoed throughout the office. Everyone heard him yelling including Darja.

"How dare you do this to your partner?" Marcel continued yelling.

Not only did Marcel and his men do the deal with Debare but Marcel rented him one of his shops to help Debare store the gold.

"Please forgive me, Marcel. Let me explain."

"If you don't get me my money by the end of the week, Kirikiri will be your new home. Do you fucking hear me?"

Marcel and the others left leaving Debare to sink in guilt. How would Debare find fifty grand in a week? *Only a miracle could save him.*

Debare packed his briefcase and left out for the

day. On his mind, as he walked through the streets; how he was going to repay Marcel.

The day went by, as Debare walked back and forth inside his flat. He lived in a place that only a government official could afford. Holding a half empty bottle of vodka, Debare was shaking.

"Why is this happening to me?"

He slammed the bottle against the wall and yelled, "Fuck!"

After hours of calling around to borrow money from those he knew, one colleague told him of a loan-shark named Shakale Oni in the red-light district.

"Shakale's usually at the Lexus Bar around 10 with his men. He won't be hard to spot; he wears an eye patch. Tell him I sent you."

The Lexus Bar was in the most dangerous neighbourhood in Lagos. It was an area known for prostitution, drugs, and robberies. The Nigerian was out of options, so he had no choice. He got dressed and lit up a cigarette. There were only a few street lights working as he walked in the night. People were looking at him weirdly as he passed by knowing he wasn't from the area.

As the Nigerian walked on, he got used to the staring. His focus was on finding the only person who might can help him; Shakale Oni. When Debare reached the Lexus, he ordered a drink.

For an hour, he waited for the man with the eyepatch to show up; drinking heavily. Debare was nervous and while he was on fifth, he saw a group of men entered, dressed in fancy suits. In the middle, stood Shakale with the leather eye patch. *Bingo!*

Debare watched as they made their way to a table. Debare put his glass down and walked over. "Shakale Oni?" The Nigerian acted as if he knew the man. Shakale looked up, agitated.

"What do the fuck do you want, man? I have no time for your kind tonight."

"I need to have a word with you. It's important."

"Not in the mood today." He waved Debare off with his hand.

Debare stood, not moving. "I am in need of something from you, sir and I'm not a beggar. I'm a businessman."

Shakale looked at Debare and the Nigerian's heart was racing. He has never been in such a desperate situation.

"Speak."

"I desire Naira from you. My friend, Oluwa told me to see you."

Shakale's men looked serious as they waited for

their boss to respond. Shakale shook his head and then smiled.

"Why did you say that from the very beginning? Sit down." Shakale pointed to a chair beside him. "How much?" asked Shakale taking a sip of Scotch while his men looked on.

"Fifty grand in US dollars."

Shakale turned to his men. His entourage dared not look back. Shakale turn back to the Nigerian and replied, "You see my men. They would never ask of me of such amount and you, a stranger has. What do you need it for, anyway?" Shakale started to believe the Nigerian was sent by the police.

"I'm in a major debt, sir. I own a jewellery shop in town and if I don't pay that amount, I'll have to close it down by month's end or sooner."

Shakale nodded, uncertain if he should give Debare the money. Yet, Debare resembled someone from the upper class.

"Who sent you again?"

"Oluwa."

"That's my man. Give me a day and you'll have it." Sipping on his Scotch, Shakale turned his attention back to the night scene. Debare exhaled thanking him.

"Matter of fact, come here first thing in the morning. Consider this your lucky day."

"Thank you, sir. Thank you."

Debare tripped over something as he got up.

Now that the Nigerian had Shakale's backing, he wanted to call Marcel. Shakale offered him a drink, but Debare declined, excusing himself to the restroom. He locked himself inside the last stall, dialling Marcel's number.

After a few rings, Marcel picked up. "What do you want!?" His voice echoed through the bathroom.

Debare cleared his throat. "I'll have your money."

Marcel paused and then chuckled. "Who did you scam this time to get my fifty grand?"

"Friday morning, I'll be at your office." Debare banged, not wanting to hear another word.

No one was in the restroom when Debare turned on the sink and splashed water on his face. He tried forgetting where he was at. It was dark and red inside with paper towels all over the floor. The Nigerian understood Shakale was more dangerous than Marcel. If he didn't return the money, Shakale would get him first.

Debare gripped the sides of the sink as the running water continued running down his face.

"Fifty grand is a lot of money--" a man said, startling Debare. The Nigerian looked in the mirror and saw a white man dressed in black standing a few feet away.

"Excuse me?"

"That's a lot of money. Am I right?"

Debare turned around. "Why were you eavesdropping on my conversation?"

"I wasn't really. I was taking a shit in this dump and overheard your boss who seems angry, huh?"

"What is it to you?"

"I know a lot of what goes on around here." The man began walking to the bathroom's exit.

Debare tried passing him but the man pushed him back.

"Well, I mean I work for people that know a lot of things that are happening around here." The man took out a gun from his back.

"Who the fuck are you? What the hell do you want?"

"Call me your fucking knight in shining armour."

"What? I have no business with you."

"I work for MI6 and I'm here to take your ass with me."

"Over my dead body."

Debare pushed him and the man pushed back, putting Debare in a chokehold. Debare tried fighting back as his eyes began rolling in the back of his head. "Let me go!" he pleaded and the man eventually did so. The Nigerian was on the ground gasping for air.

"What do you want? I have no money," said the Nigerian struggling to catch his breath. The man kneeled beside him and pointed his gun to Debare's head, "I can turn you in and you'll rot in Kirikiri until you fucking die."

"Please don't."

"Get up, you piece of shit!"

With his hands on the back of his head, Debare got up sweating.

"Now, do as I say. No questions or else." The man grabbed his phone and dialled. "Unless you want to walk out here naked, it's your fucking choice."

Debare didn't say anything further. As they were exiting, Debare looked around to see if Shakale was still around, but it appeared that he left. Once outside, a black van screeched pulling up to and the white man pushed Debare inside.

"Listen, I borrowed money from one of the most dangerous men in Nigeria at that bar. At least, let me take care of my problem."

"I'll fix your problems. Just enjoy the ride. We have a long flight ahead of us."

"WELCOME, TO THE UNITED KINGDOM," A service agent said, welcoming everyone off the plane.

Just a day ago, Debare was almost ready to pay off Marcel and now he's thousands of miles away. His fate was either spend the rest of his life in Kirikiri or die at the hands of Shakale and Marcel. *Why the fuck am I even here?* Debare was given an address and told to say nothing.

The flight was nine hours, and Debare couldn't sleep. It was the first time in years since he boarded an airplane. He dragged his suitcase through airport customs and then on towards the exit.

A cab driver waiting for his next fare spotted Debare. "Hey, my friend. Get inside."

Debare gave the address to the driver and while on the road, he didn't speak.

The fog and cloudy skies of London surprised Debare. He snapped a few photos with a new phone given to him. It had only a few apps and one contact in case of an emergency. "We're minutes away."

"Thank you, sir." Debare nodded, saying nothing else. The Nigerian was eager to see what he got himself into.

Five minutes later, the driver said, "We're here."

Debare paid and got out. The building in front was huge and constructed futuristically. He went to the gate and found it locked. There was an intercom on the side. He pushed the button and an old woman answered.

"Military Intelligence 6, how may I help you?"

"My name's Debare Balogun from Nigeria. I was told to report here by one of your agents."

"Your name again is?"

"Debare Balogun."

The gate buzzed. There was a long driveway leading up to the main entrance. Unmarked black and white cars were parked on both sides of the driveway.

Debare entered and saw people in suits engaged in what appeared to be operations. The receptionist stared at him and figured he was lost.

"May I help you?"

Debare turned as if he didn't hear her. "Oh, oh. "I

was told to come inside, and I'm clueless about where to begin."

"You're Debare Balogun. Am I correct?" She asked looking at her computer.

"That would be me." Debare nodded while scratching the back of his head.

"The general is expecting you on Level 5, Office 230." The lady smiled and handed him a visitor's pass to access the elevator.

The elevator was crowded, and no one went to the fifth floor except Debare. He got off and walked down a dark empty hallway to Office 230. There were voices talking when Debare knocked.

Then there was a silence before someone yelled, "Come in."

Debare walked in, seeing men and women dressed in military fatigue. They appeared to be the high-ranking police but none were wearing badges or name tags.

"Good day, gentleman."

"And who you might be?" an old man yelled from afar. Debare turned and saw him sitting and thought he was in charge.

"Debare Balogun, sir." Debare straighten himself as if he was ready to salute.

Everyone turned their attention to the Nigerian.

Debare waited for the old man to respond but was kept in suspense because he didn't quickly.

"Well, we've been expecting you. Ladies and Gentlemen, please if you have work to do, take it to your areas."

A few got up and left while some others took seats at a round table in the room's center.

"I am General Robert Wilson. Have a seat, Mr Balogun. Did I pronounce your name correctly."

"Yes, you did, sir."

Debare tried sitting at the farthest place from the General, almost tripping over some cables. The general stood up, opened a drawer and took out some files.

"Why am I here, sir, if you don't mind me asking?"

"Why are you here? This lad is funny." The group of agents laughed and General Wilson chuckled.

"With your history of fraud, we thought you'd be the perfect candidate for this operation," Robert walked over to the table and handed some files to Debare. "Let's just say I have chosen you for something very important that requires your expertise."

Debare looked over the papers seeing that were numerous charts and stats he couldn't understand. "What are these, sir?"

"Russia's making a lot of money. They have the strongest economy in Europe and Asia."

Debare crossed his arms.

"I'll say this again, Russia has the highest GDP today," said Robert, having second thoughts. Debare was more focused on the papers then what the General had to say.

"There's no coincidence that their GDP has skyrocketed. Thieves like yourself use Russia's black market all the time. Am I correct?"

"Maybe."

"Don't fucking maybe me, Debare. I know you fucking criminals like the back of my hand. Fucking diamonds in Nigeria are replicas for these Russians. That's why Marcel Verhoeff wants his money back. There's no collusion, I guess."

Everyone laughed.

"Tell me. Are you up for a mission, son?"

"It depends."

"It depends on your life. You are trying to say?"

Debare was puzzled.

General Wilson continued, "Last week, Russia was all over the fake news because two Cullinan diamonds were located at the Popigai Crater".

As General spoke, Debare wondered how It was even possible. There were only less than ten found in the world.

We estimate "One Cullinan diamond's worth to be around two billion dollars."

The amount took aback Debare. The others listened while typing on their laptops.

"Debare, we need you to go to Russia as a refugee and see what's going on. We need to know the truth about whether these diamonds are in good hands or bad pockets."

Debare's heart raced as he learned about what his role would be. If he refused, he would eat bean soup in Kirikiri for life or killed.

"Sir, I'm not so—"

"Well, you have no other choice. I'm not asking."

The other agents stared at Debare as if they were ordered to imprison him if he didn't follow along. The Nigherian nodded slowly and one agent signalled for Debare to follow.

"You will be changing identities for the mission and your past will be forever lost," explained Robert as Debare was getting up.

"Our agent, Brian will give you all the details, so don't let us down, Debare. This is what we Brits call "life or death." Debare noticed the white man from the club, waiting at the door.

The Nigerian was no longer in charge of his destiny. This mission had no guarantees. What would happen to his business in Lagos? Marcel and Shakale? His secretary Daraja? Debare had so many twists and very little answers.

His stay in the United Kingdom was brief. Ever since he was a boy, he always wanted to visit London. Now when he had the chance, it was under duress. This was no vacation. His life was hanging in balance by MI6. Debare left the building with Brian after getting briefed for hours. The Nigerian was in a black van on his way to Heathrow Airport. Brian gave him an extra suitcase telling him not to open it until he landed in Moscow. He was also told there was one satellite phone inside. MI6 instructed not to make any calls unless ordered.

Debare wasn't close to his family but asked Brian to allow him to leave them a message just in case something happened. The order was granted, so he texted his mother:

"I miss you terribly, Mama. I'm away on business. I hope my absence doesn't worry you. Mama! You'll hear from me soon. Love, Debare."

His greed for money made him grow apart from his family. They couldn't have their own being a fraudster. They knew Debare's transactions were dishonest, but still, they called begging him for money when they were in trouble.

Made to believed the Nigerian was headed to the

airport, the driver diverted off to a secret military aircraft hanger. From there, Debare boarded a plane along with a few other men. The estimated flight time to Moscow was three hours and thirty-five minutes. Everyone was told not to speak.

There were strong patches of turbulence throughout the flight. The small plane rocked back and forth for hours scaring everyone. When it finally landed, there were cheers and whistling. Debare got off with two suitcases and observed they were at a makeshift airstrip. The snow was falling heavily, and he was confused about where to go next. One man nudged him and pointed at a truck ahead. The passengers hurried inside, and in the heavy snow, the truck didn't leave any traces.

***

While moving, Debare received a text stating, "St. Hemmingway 13, a group of refugees are gathered, ready to speak to the Minister. Be there."

The instructions were confusing. The passengers were silent as the truck arrived in Moscow within the hour. Debare was dropped off across the street from the UK consulate. The snow was lighter in Moscow. A man met him outside and took one of his suitcases. Debare didn't ask questions watching the man go back inside. The Nigerian started his phone's GPS to find St. Hemmingway 13.

It was a fifteen-minute walk and Debare was out of breath as he walked through the snow. The combination of jetlag and little exercise didn't help. He didn't know where he'd lodge but knew he had to hurry. When Debare arrived, there was a group of Africans in front of a building, protesting. He was at the right place and joined the crowd, pushing his way through to almost the front. 'The Federal Assembly' was engraved in the building's front.

A small batch of Russians walked out and stood at the podium minutes later. One man began speaking in broken English.

"Today is a day of celebration, I'm here to say I stand with you!" The man raised his fist. Everyone in the crowd cheered. "I am deeply saddened by the fact you are forced to flee your countries' violence and poverty and now you are being exploited to greater harm; trafficking, prostitution, and persecution. I'm here to say as long as I'm a part of this Parliament, you're welcomed to our country!"

As the demonstration went on, Debare lost focus until his phone texted: "These are the profiles of the people standing on the platform."

Dabare skimmed through them quickly, seeing they were all part of the Parliament. Debare assumed

MI6 was there with him. As long as drones exist, the man is always looking in. A man next to the speaker caught the Nigerian's attention. He appeared to be in charge of Russia's high-end nightclubs according to his profile. How does this man have time to run them while working in Parliament?

His phone buzzed again. "Follow Boris Petrov once the speech is over."

Debare waited patiently. T-shirts, food, and water were handed out from volunteers. Why are they giving out T-shirts in minus-5 temperatures? Debare's phone buzzed again. "Put the tracker inside his suitcase."

The crowd began clearing out, and Debare saw Boris leaving alongside with his bodyguards and the other Parliament members. He took out the tracker from his bag and held it tightly. As he was catching up to Boris, he played out what he wanted to do in his head.

"Sir Petrov!"

Boris turned around with his men.

"Something fell out of your suitcase!"

"What may it be?" he asked as Debare came closer. One of Boris' bodyguards tried blocking his way.

Boris appeared annoyed. "This is your pen." Boris took it from Debare placing it in his suitcase. "Your work in helping us refugees is highly appreciated. Thank you, sir." Boris shook the Nigerian's hand and then proceeded with his entourage to an unmarked car.

The sunshine came out as Debare walked through the streets in the direction of the UK consulate. When the Nigerian reached, he received a call from an unknown number, telling him the next steps of his mission.

CHAPTER ELEVEN_

DEBARE'S STATION was already set up allowing him to tap into Boris Petkov's tracker and listen when he arrived home. Boris' conversations were boring as the interpreter's voice made the Nigeria fall asleep at times. All he talked about was the hot chicks he had, the whisky he drank and an upcoming meeting with Putin he was looking forward to. Roughly into the second hour, Debare was interrupted by a phone call from an unknown number again.

"Hello?"

Then there was a long pause.

"You shouldn't have shown your face, Debare."

It was Brian. The Nigerian rolled his eyes as he looked inside the fridge seeing it was full.

"Well, how was I supposed to get to him without the fucker seeing me?"

"Don't give me that shit, you dumb fuck."

"Give me an order that's clear or I'll do it how I like."

"Do you want to go home to Kirikiri? Watch your mouth." Brian hanged up.

"Doko mi," shouted Debare in Yoruba which means "suck my dick."

Just when Debare was about to throw the phone against the wall, the sound of a phone rang on the feed streaming Boris. Debare pressed the button on his laptop to read the English interpretation.

"Where are the diamonds? I need my money right away," pleaded Boris.

A man on the line was calculating prices. "They've already sold two, sir, and the cash was deposited."

The call ended, and Boris went to the bathroom to take a shit. Debare stopped the feed. Other two, huh? That meant the Russians dug up four at the Popigai Crater instead of two. He rushed to call Brian back and he took a long time to answer.

"I've got news for you. The diamonds are four not two, sir."

"What? But there were only two according to our intel? Then, the other two will--."

Brian appeared to be proud of the Nigerian now. "Hmm. Listen, tonight you'll need to sneak inside the

Ministry of Finance building. There's one man named Aleksandar Andreev. Get inside his office and gather whatever Intel you can. I will send you a file briefing you on what we are looking for specifically." Debare listened while biting down his nails.

"Yes, sir," replied Debare and then he hung up. Debare rolled the recording, again and again, looking for anything else until he became sleepy. Tonight, Mr Balogun will start his first true mission.

* * *

Two hours had passed and Debare was ready. He walked out on the streets, dressed in an ushanka (fur hat) and black fur coat. It was cold as hell as he approached the Metro station. It will be his first time taking the train. Back in Lagos, no one who had money had patience to be cramped up with hundreds on Nigeria's daily commute. Some even hired helicopters to escape the dreaded traffic.

At 10 PM, the train was packed; each passenger was pushing one another trying to get a seat. Debare sat and wondered what nightlife they had if they were working so much on the weekdays.

After a few stations, he got off at Kursky Station. The Nigerian lit up a cigarette and strolled toward the Ministry of Finance in the Siberian cold. Once the Nigerian spotted the monumental building, he plotted how he would sneak inside. There were two guards out front, holding AK 47s. Debare stood farther resembling a homeless man looking for a place to stay.

He encircled the building to the back entrance. It was locked with a security camera moving overhead. Brian texted him, "I will take care of the cameras and door."

Seconds later, the cameras shut off, and the door beeped. The halls inside were dark and the Nigerian put on his night-vision glasses. He took a right to the stairs leading to the top floor. Debare's footsteps were flat matching a professional burglar.

When Debare turned up a hallway, he bumped into the night janitor. The Nigerian's heart raced as he was dumbfounded.

"Hey, what are you doing here?" the man said in Russian.

Debare grabbed the old man, choking him to sleep. He then hit him on the back of the head with his gun's butt to finish the job. Debare dragged him to the nearest maintenance closet and put him inside.

"Get to Aleksandar's office without fucking getting caught," whispered Brian in Debare's earpiece.

"Yes, sir."

The last floor was where the Minister's office was located. Brian didn't have Intel on a specific room number and Debare knew he had to get there some-time tonight. After passing a few offices, the Nigerian focused his attention on the last door down the hall which appeared newly constructed. He scanned the name on the door with his phone, and the phone's translation came up with Aleksandar's name. Debare turned the knob, but it was locked. Looking behind, he opened his sac and grabbed two metal pins. After a few seconds, the Nigerian got the door open and felt proud; reflecting his scamming for years had finally paid off.

He shut the door and searched Aleksandar's drawers for anything tied to the Diamonds. There were Playboy magazines and other documents but nothing. He put his hands on his head and blurted "Odi Oshi" which means "stupid fuck." Moments later, the Nigerian accidentally knocked over a lamp. Someone rushed down the hall and Debare hid in a closet. Aleksandar's door opened slightly and a security guard peeped inside with his flashlight.

"Is anyone in here?" the guard said in Russian. He came closer to the closet but didn't open it. He then circled the room, finding the broken lamp on the ground. "Let maintenance handle this shit. Damn, rats again!" The guard closed the door.

Debare waited for a bit before coming out. He was determined to find the files. On the other side of the room, was a safe with a keypad. "They have to be inside."

Debare kneeled taking out talc powder from his sac and spread it lightly around the keypad and brushed upwards, leaving little traces along the buttons. After two failed attempts, the safe was cracked. There were rubles, sex toys, and folders inside. His eyes grew when he saw the bills. There had to be thousands of rubles. "Don't touch the money. I know you," alerted Brian from the earpiece.

The Nigerian took snapshots of the files, checking them although they were in Russian. The last one caught his eye. There was an invoice from yesterday in the range of 4 billion dollars. Taking a clear photo, Debare sent it to Brian. Perhaps it was the money from the two missing Cullinan?

The Nigerian's phone buzzed right away and it was Brian. "Track the individuals involved in the transactions and take any evidence back with you." Debare instantly felt like a real spy.

He placed a mini-recorder underneath the desk, grabbed some folders and left. Creeping down the halls, Debare made it out undetected. When he got home, Boris was chatting on his live feed.

"This activist is in on the fraud as well," mumbled Debare.

Another text message from Brian came in. "Meet

me at City Space in thirty minutes. Don't be late." Debare changed, came back out and entered the location on the app. "It's cold as a motherfucker out here," said Debare lighting up a cigarette as he closed the door behind.

* * *

City Space is one of the most popular bars in Moscow at the city's tallest building known as the Vostok Towers. Debare arrived early, waiting for Brian at a table near the back. People were dancing, drinking and having a good time as Moscow never sleeps. Debare ordered a Scotch and watched crowds of beautiful women resembling supermodels jam the dancefloor. A few minutes later, Brian showed up.

"You did well." Brian admitted not looking at Debare while calling over a waiter.

"Finally, Brian."

"Who told you, you can call me by my first name?"

"Myself," Debare said sipping on his drink.

"Enough of this blabbering and let's get down to work. Here, take this."

Brian handed Debare a folder with a picture of a middle-aged woman clipped on the front. The name 'Alina Grekova' was written in black underneath it. Debare glanced inside as the waiter came back with Brian's drink.

"I'm ready."

"The woman in the picture is the Minister of Education." Brian sipped while flipping the folder's pages for Debare. "And here are some of her felonious activities."

The words 'Drug trafficking, prostitution, human trafficking' caught Debare's eye.

"How did she become the Minister of Education?"

Brian sidestepped Debare's question. "Alina's a brunette with bangs that hang low over her forehead. They say her grandmother dropped her when she was a baby. The bangs cover the large gash. She's originally from Poland but moved here with her daughter. Some say her daughter's a drug addict, and that's the reason they came to Moscow."

Brian took a long sip and then finished:

"The point being Alina Grekova is involved in all types of shit. Believe me! Tomorrow, the Parliament will hold their final session before taking a break for the holidays. I'm positive she'll be there. Follow her after the session closes and find out who she'll be meeting with. Familiarise yourself with her past and get some rest".

Brian got up and strolled out, leaving Debare to pay the tab. "Omo Ale (Bastard)," shouted Debare.

Debare went home a few hours later and tried digging up anything he could on Alina Grekova. There wasn't much online except for a few articles on how well she's done with the kindergartens. There was also an article of her posing with some local high-school students at a hockey game. Debare closed his laptop and went to bed.

CHAPTER TWELVE

"It's too early in the morning for this shit," conceived the Nigerian as he reached the Metro station. The journey was thirty minutes long and there weren't any empty seats. Debare held on and after a few stops, he decided to get off to grab some coffee. He didn't realise it would be a twenty-five-minute walk to the Kremlin Senate from his location. After arriving, he stood by a bench near the front entrance and took snapshots. Minutes later, a few unmarked government cars arrived in and a few senior officials got out, embracing one another. Debare spotted Alina Grekova in the last one, greeting her colleagues. She hugged them and then they proceeded inside. Alina was dressed up as if she was attending a holiday party.

"Something big is going on."

Her driver walked away and went to take a break

with the others. They chatted and smoked not far from their vehicles. Debare crept up to Alina's, took some snapshots and placed a tracker underneath. Once he came up, a man startled him. "What are you doing here?"

"I don't know Russian, sir. I'm a tourist and I love this car," said Debare staring at the others all wearing black suits with matching black shoes.

"I've always wanted to buy a car like this. Do you know who's the owner?"

The driver shook his head trying to make out Debare's accent. Moments later, he responded.

"I do. She's the Minister of Education. By the way, man, I like your country America. You have the fucking hottest chicks."

"Thank you." Debare chuckled.

The driver looked over at his colleagues who were now looking and suddenly changed facial expressions.

"I must ask you to leave right away."

"Okay, man. You got a cool car here! Remember to come see us in America. You'll get a hot chick."

The driver saluted and the Nigerian walked off.

Debare received a text from Brian stating the meeting was in progress and to wait around until it concluded. The Nigerian smoked a few cigarettes while strolling through the area. An hour later, Brian texted him, "There's a motorcycle parked behind the

Senate for you. License plate number: H647xCC-77. Its keys are in the left jacket."

Ninety minutes passed and Debare received a text stating the Ministers were coming out exchanging their goodbyes. Alina proceed to get in the car with an unknown man. The Nigerian put on his helmet and followed. Keeping his distance, they drove through downtown Moscow; passing by many high-end restaurants and strip clubs. Alina's car finally stopped at Turandot. Debare took snapshots as Alina kissed this unknown man in public.

"That guy must be her lover."

The two lovebirds walked inside and Debare parked across the street. The Nigerian then proceeded to the restaurant's front and was stopped. "Do you have a reservation, sir?" the clerk said in broken English.

"No, I do not but I need to get in. It's cold and I have a friend coming."

"I am sorry sir but that's not possible. You'll need a reservation and can come in when your friend arrives."

The clock resumed his work when Debare pulled out a hundred-dollar bill and placed it on top of the desk.

"I'm sure you can find an empty table and a glass of

wine for a dear friend?"

"Let me escort you right in. Come right this way, sir. Hurry, it's cold out."

Debare followed and the restaurant was nearly empty.

"Here you are. Your drink will be up shortly."

Debare looked over the menu, seated not far away from Alina. A waiter came over a few moments later asking for his order.

"The cheapest thing," said Debare swatting the waiter away. Alina's lover pulled out a huge ring and placed it on her finger. Her face lit up as she repeatedly kissed him. Debare took a few snapshots and waited calmly for his order.

A text came on his screen: "Hack Alina's phone. I just upload a virus to yours. Open the NFC and get close."

Minutes later, Alina got up and went to the restroom. The Nigerian got up at the same time and went over to her table and sat.

"That's a lovely suit, sir. Where did you get it from?" Debare said staring at Alina's handbag.

"Excuse me, who are you? You're in my lady's seat." The man spoke in broken English.

"I work for the VIP," pointed Debare to his right, intentionally flipping over the handbag. Alina's phone fell out and Debare reached for it.

"So sorry, sir. I'll pick up everything."

Debare stooped and put his phone on top of Alina's. The program took a few seconds to start, and it began counting by percentages. "Uploading 35%."

"What the hell are you doing?" the man said standing up.

"The makeup spilled all over, sir. She has a lot of beauty products."

"Now at 50%," read the screen. Debare pulled the table cloth causing the wine to stain the man's pants. The man ran away to the restroom to get the stain off. Debare's phone now was reading, "80%." Debare heard the sound of Alina's high heels approaching.

"95%."

"Oh shit!" gasped Debare.

Alina arrived. "What's going on here? Why are my things on the floor?" she said in Russian.

"100%."

Debare stood up handing Alina her handbag and straightened himself up. "Sorry lady, I don't speak Russian. You have some fine beauty products. Take care and have a pleasant evening."

"Thank you, sir." Alina was astonished not knowing what happened.

Debare left a one-hundred-dollar bill for the man to clean his suit and then rode off.

"It's done." Debare texted Brian.

"Good, now you can check her phone history and eavesdrop on her lovely chats."

"Alina's in love."

"With whom?"

"I think it's with a minister. He wasn't there at the refugee rally. I don't know who he is."

"Find out."

Brian hung up the phone down and yelled, "Fuck."

Back home, Debare began tracking Alina while having Boris and Aleksandar on the split-screen monitor. With the help of the MI6, he wrote every number that appeared on Alina's phone. There was a person named Andrei Trubanov, the acting Minister of Finance who frequently called. He was present at the refugee rally. Debare glimpsed through her photo gallery looking for more evidence on her activities. He found many photos of her daughter and family. However, there was one that showed a large diamond resembling one of the Cullinans.

"Alina's in on the heist. Are the entire cabinet colluding as well?"

For hours, he replayed Boris's tracker for more details. In his notes, Debare wrote: "It appears the last diamond was last supervised by Boris. One diamond was sold so far, and the statesmen divided the profits. Alina was the first to receive a payment according to the invoice found in Aleksandar's office. Aleksandar was paid, but it doesn't mention when. He also has strong ties with Alina in a few businesses. There are five more suspects to investigate." Debare marked the remaining seven ministers at the rally that day for further probes and sent his report to Brian.

Around 9 AM the next morning, the Nigerian's phone had awakened him. It was Brian. "I got you in one of the parliament meetings as a security guard, be there in 30. Your uniform's in janitor closet A." Debare jumped out of bed and showered.

The Nigerian made it to the Senate building in 20. It was cold outside and only a few dared to come out to smoke. Debare entered the back entrance through the garage and had trouble finding the janitor's closet. After circling around the building, he found it and shut himself inside. He found the security uniform folded on a chair and an earpiece. The Nigerian quickly got dressed, fixing his hat and placed a small camera on his collar. "This shirt looks good." Debare still didn't know what room the meeting was being held in.

"Hey! Buddy," yelled Debare, approaching a fat security guard at the end of the hall. "Do you speak English?"

"Yes."

"Where's the meeting? They have me stationed nearby just in case, someone spills their drink."

"Haha, in Hall Room—. Wait, a minute. I haven't seen you before. Have I?" The guard hobbled towards Debare.

"Yeah, I've been around. Just been sick lately, but this is my first day back."

The guard paused. "Hmm, you're Peter from Sudan?"

"Yes, sir."

"Now I remember. Vladislav told me about you the other day, you can go. It's right down in Hall Room B."

"I never heard of anyone named Peter from Africa," whispered Debare to himself.

As Debare drew closer, he spotted Alina talking to Boris outside the door. Debare lowered his head and passed by. A dozen government officials were seated. Alina laughed as she entered inside with Boris. Once they sat, the two kept chatting until the meeting started. Debare heard the sound check in his earpiece for the language interpretation.

***

The clock in the room read ten, and the ministers' meeting is now in session. As others came in almost late, two security guards had closed the doors and instructed Debare and his co-guard to keep quiet. An older man was seated at the head of the table started speaking. "Ladies," he said pointing at Alina and "Gentlemen," while smiling at the rest. "As you may know, Russia is now the leading economic powerhouse in all of Europe and Asia. All thanks to our friend, Boris."

The speaker started clapping and the others followed along. "Let's say, Vlad had a major role in transferring the diamonds."

Who's Vlad? There was no intel on that name.

The speaker continued, "Vlad will come back home from his trip shortly."

"I think we should throw him a party," shouted one minister. Everyone cheered, but Alina and Boris stayed silent looking agitated.

"Anyway, let's get to work, shall we? With our growing economy, many companies from abroad want to invest in our country nowadays. We have to take advantage of the momentum. You, the ministers, will be in charge of the areas of our incoming investments." Everyone present gave him their undivided attention.

Meanwhile, Debare observed Alina and Boris' body language keeping his head down, so they wouldn't recognise him.

The speaker went on to continue. "Collectively,

twenty of the world's biggest companies want to invest in our country so there will be fifty thousand jobs which would make our economy even stronger. We'd like a twenty-year commitment from each, guaranteeing that they'll not take our money and just run." Everyone clapped except for Alina and Boris.

"Shouldn't we first offer small contracts for 2 to 3 years to see how they do?" interrupted Alina raising her hand.

"We are in no position to negotiate at this time. It's either take-it-or-leave-it."

"I mean twenty foreign corporations seems like a stretch operating at one time in our country without adequate oversight. They'll have enormous revenue being that Russia's taxes are currently the lowest in 25 years."

"Alina, look at the bright side, over fifty thousand Russian citizens will have good-paying jobs. We wouldn't have to worry about them going abroad supporting other nations' economies," stated the head minister while flipping through papers. "And we will have first-hand knowledge about the interests of these corporations before they're made public."

The speaker had a history of out-talking Alina which caused her to keep quiet as another minister stood up. "With the growing economy and these latest developments, I think we need to raise the workers' salary to about fifteen percent for the forthcoming year."

Debare recognised him from the rally. It was the Minister of Finance, Aleksandar Andreev.

Most approved the notion and clapped. Alina rose shouting, "Absolutely not! This will bring down our country in less than six months."

"Alina, calm down 15 percent isn't that much. I think we can handle it with the new investors coming in. A happy country is a safe one. No one will question what is being done behind the scenes as long as they are happy."

"This is crazy. The economic forecast of adding fifteen percent will raise our budget so quickly that it will crash our stock markets to the ground. There will be a recession and businesses would pack up and leave Russia. I see we're not on the same page here, Minister," said Boris sharply.

The president of the Parliament interjected and said, "I am in support of this motion, and I'll leave it for you all to vote on it in our next assembly after the break."

Alina grabbed her purse and left out in a rage, leaving the door open. She rushed pass Debare, not recognising him. After she left, the session recommenced, and there were a few more things on the table. A few more disputes took place between Boris and the rest of the council. By the end, everyone seemed frustrated with one another and was ready to go on break.

Debare's headed for the front gate. The same security spotted Debare passing through again and stopped him. "Excuse me, sir. Who are you again?" Alongside him was a man of African descent dressed in the same uniform.

"I'm Peter, sir."

"But, Peter's right here with me. You're an imposter. Come with me right away." The supervisor ordered Peter to stand put while he dealt with the Nigerian.

As they were heading to his office, Debare told him to look down because the old man dropped something.

The guard looked and Debare tripped him. The Nigerian ran as fast as he could to the exit passing by the African and out the door. The real Peter stood there laughing.

"Stop him. Stop him. You dumb fool!"

Peter raised his arms as the old man ran past him into an elderly woman who just entered.

"Hello, my son. I need directions," asked the old woman.

Out of respect, the old man stopped and answered giving Debare more than enough time to escape.

"I can't believe you did that! Are you out of your fucking mind?" yelled Brian inside Debare's flat.

The Nigerian was drunk; replaying in his cognizance what happened earlier. He wasn't in the mood for Brian's schoolboy lectures.

The Senate Building breach was the top story of the hour. Luckily, Debare's face wasn't identifiable, but footage showed a black male running out. Brian knew this may compromise the mission, and if it were up to him, he would have pulled Debare out at once.

"What do you have to say for yourself?" Brian hit the table earning very little attention from Debare.

"I made a mistake, don't we all?"

"You cannot afford to make mistakes as a spy. I told you not to get caught, but you did the exact opposite."

Debare sighed. "The old man caught me leaving. Your Intel sucks. I was supposed to be in the clear."

"You are on a mission and trained to avoid detection."

"What's my next mission then? I'll do a better job next time."

"Oh! Your next mission? Don't even fucking bother." Brian spat toward Debare. "Robert assigned another agent, so MI6 won't be needing you any longer."

"Oh my god! I'm ruined. I deserve a second chance. I don't want to Kirikiri."

Brian didn't say anything right away. He sat down on the couch and watched more of the news coverage while having himself a drink. Debare in the meantime vomited. Brian carried him to the bathroom and leaned him over the toilet.

Brian cared about his agents and didn't accept any mistakes. Mistakes mean dead lives. He accepted that he might have picked the wrong person. Debare came out, barely able to walk and sat down next to Brian.

"Sober up, I've got a quick assignment for you."

The Nigerian looked pitiful and Brian felt a bit remorseful on how he spoke to Debare.

"Listen up! Alina Grekova's daughter, Gala is hosting a party at the Night Flight; a popular club here.

All you will need is VIP access." Brian scrolled through his phone, searching for something.

"How will I get in?"

"I'll take care of it but you must look presentable." Brian looked at him from his head to his toe. "Pick out the best you have. I'll have your access in a few hours."

"And Debare, don't fuck this up."

Midnight came, and it was time for Debare to leave. He rode his bike downtown and within minutes, found the club. Crowds were in line, waiting to go inside. Debare walked up to the bouncers and they looked skeptically at him but when the Nigerian flashed his VIP ticket, they made room for him to go inside.

He ignored the stares of the Russian chaps and sat down near the bar. Techno music was playing and everyone on the dance floor was jumping up and down.

"What would you like to order, sir?"

"A beer.".

While the Nigerian waited, he examined Gala's picture on his phone. How was he going to approach her without looking like a creep? The Nigerian looked older than most of those partying.

"Here you are, sir."

Moments later, Debare spotted Gala. Her beauty

was stunning. Then, she disappeared into the crowd. The Nigerian looked up to see if she was on the second floor. She wasn't there but popped up dancing with the crowd on the first. Debare took a sip of his beer not pulling his eyes away from her.

"Do you need anything else?" interrupted the bartender.

"No, thanks," Debare smirked, turning his attention back to Gala. He wondered if Gala knew her mother was deceiving the citizens as being the Minister of Education.

Minutes later, she approached the bar, leaning close to Debare. He smelled her heavy perfume. "A Tequila, please."

Debare watched her chuck it down. Her friends ran over and cheered, yelling her name. This scene reminded him when he was hanging out all over Lagos. Drinking friendships don't last forever, and Debare forgot most of his friends once he started his business.

"Hey, bartender. Do you speak English?"

"Yes, I studied it in school."

"Who is that girl over there?"

"Oh! Believe me, you don't want her," said the bartender while serving other patrons.

"I wonder why?"

"She's the bratty Minister's daughter. She only hangs out with rich boys."

"So that means I have no chance?"

"Probably not. She's in a league by herself."

Debare was instructed to tail her, and not to do anything crazy. This mission was quite boring but it was Debare's chance to redeem himself. Meantime, Gala started dancing with two guys who were grinding against her. Her skimpy outfit looked like it cost a fortune. The young girl kept coming to the bar every few minutes ordering more drinks. The Nigerian took more snapshots of her dancing erotically and looking at her wasn't a waste of time.

Another woman who was more beautiful than Gala came in. She almost pushed Debare off the stool to sit down. She danced and moved provocatively as waited for her drink. Her body was mesmerising and Debare kept looking at her ass. Whoever she was, she could have been a fashion model. Minutes later, she accidentally tripped over the big stool in front of her, spilling her drink on Dabare. The Nigerian was grateful he was wearing black.

"Oh my God, I'm so sorry!" The woman grabbed a napkin from the counter dabbing it on Debare's shirt.

Debare grabbed the napkin from her hand and tried doing it himself. The woman apologised over and over, but Debare kept saying it was okay.

"I don't even know what I was looking at."

Debare looked at her and then to her bosoms,

seeing a rather odd rock resembling a diamond; lying perfectly in the center. It looked like the Cullinan but no one could tell.

"Come with me over to my table, I'll make it up for you." The lady smiled and it left Debare puzzled.

Debare didn't want to miss out the opportunity. The woman grabbed the Nigerian by the hand and pulled him through the center towards the elite VIP section. At her table, were two other men about her age who looked like they were her bodyguards.

"What's your name?" the woman hummed in the Nigerian's ear, licking her lips.

"Peter."

"I'm Nikita."

"Nice to meet you, Nikita." The men at the table didn't introduce themselves and stared at Debare. "This is Evgeni, and that's Nikolai." Again, none of them greeted.

"Good evening, gentlemen."

"Okay, well do you want something to drink?"

"I think I've had enough for tonight." Debare looked away trying to spot Gala, but she wasn't around.

"What's wrong, baby?"

"Nothing. About that drink you offered, I've changed my mind." Nikita handed him a glass of vodka.

"Cheers!"

Nikita watched Debare chuck it down in one shot. "Why are you here alone, baby?" Nikita whispered over the loud music.

"My friends, they left earlier," said Debare looking at her bosoms. It was one of the Cullinans but how so?

"Well, I'm not letting you leave soon, now that your friends are gone." Her hands rubbed down his chest, making little gestures with her fingers. The Nigerian wanted to laugh. He never met a woman like this, driven with such tenacity yet classy. Her movements were alluring. The Nigerian watched her seductively moving her ass as she called him over to the dance floor, wiggling her finger. Debare looked seeing everyone dancing except for her two bodyguards. Nikita quickly wrapped her arms around the Nigerian and he could feel her warm breath on his neck. He then wrapped his arms around her waist, still trying to locate Gala to no avail.

"Sorry about Nikolai and Evgeni. They're not very nice to strangers."

"It's fine, I'm still here because of you." The Nigerian kept looking at her bosoms.

The song changed to an upbeat track, and Nikita let Debare go. She went over to Nikolai and Evgeni, forcing them to dance with her. Debare sat, sipping on his drink watching the action for a few minutes.

"I'm going to the bathroom, sweetheart." Debare felt Nikita's hand on his head. He put his drink down smiling, looking at her ass as she was walking away.

"I'll be back and you don't go nowhere," Nikita yelled before disappearing. Her bodyguards, Nikolai and Evgeni then walked up to Debare angrily.

"What's your business with Nikita!?" said Nikolai.

"Excuse me?"

"You heard my friend, what do you want from Nikita?" demanded Evgeni. The Nigerian kept his composure.

"Nothing, she invited me over to pay me back for ruining my shirt."

"You have jokes, huh?"

Evgeni balled his fists, but Nikolai grabbed him. "Stay away from her," said Evgeni, but Debare just shrugged.

"Tell Nikita that. I'm only here for tonight."

The two picked up their things from the table and appeared to be leaving. Debare didn't give them no attention and continued sipping his drink. Moments later, Nikita rejoined the Nigerian and took a seat. "Where are Nikolai and Evgeni?"

"They left early, I guess and didn't want to say goodbye."

Nikita rolled her eyes. "I didn't like them anyway. My father sent them to protect me," explained Nikita roaming through her bag. "I'm not feeling well, Peter." Her eyes started closing as if she was about to faint.

"What's wrong?"

"I think I might have been poisoned," slurred Nikita.

The men responsible for protecting her were trying to kill her. It was almost three in the morning. The night club was packed, and it looked like the party wasn't anywhere close to ending. When Debare got up to help, gunshots were heard from the front entrance. Everybody screamed, and the music was still playing. Nikita came back to her senses.

"Nikita! We know you're in here. Just give up!" A man screamed loudly.

"We don't want that pretty little face of yours to get hurt now, do we!?" Another man yelled in Russian.

Debare carried Nikita and tried his best not to get caught under the flashing lights.

"There she is! Get her!" Debare thrust Nikita to run. People were yelling and they ran by and headed towards the back. When they made it outside, Nikita said, "There's my car, the keys are inside." She pointed at an expensive black Mercedes at the end of the parking lot.

"Stop right there!" Debare looked back.

A gunman pointed at Nikita and was about to pull the trigger. Debare saw he couldn't help, so he jumped in front of her. The gunman fired and the bullet struck Debare's leg.

"Oh, God! It hurts."

Nikita drew her gun out and shot the man in the head. "Fucking bitch," yelled Nikita as she knelt to assist Debare.

She shouldered him inside the car and drove to the nearest hospital as Debare was losing lots of blood. Nikita pulled Debare out and shouldered him towards the reception.

"Help me, please! This man has been shot."

Others sitting down, who were more worried than Nikita, got up out of their seats to give Debare a place. His blood was splattered on the white hospital floors from the entrance to the seating area.

"What happened!?" A doctor came running up, inspecting Debare.

"Someone shot him in the leg! He's losing blood!"

"Nurse, prepare the operating room. This one can't wait."

"Yes, Doctor. Right away."

Two nurses shouldered Debare and the doctor told Nikita to wait in the lobby. She put her hands on her head and was visibly shaken. An old woman came from behind and comforted her telling Nikita everything will be okay.

Nikita waited in front of Debare's hospital room; waiting for the doctors to give her permission to go inside. Last evening, they removed the bullet from his leg, which just missed breaking his tibia. The Nigerian's pain was so unbearable that the doctors told her to come back in the morning.

She left but returned, being the first visitor to arrive at the hospital in the morning.

"You can go in now." A nurse told her.

Nikita walked in closing the door finding Debare awake.

"Hey!" said Debare seeing her enter. He tried sitting up but struggled and Nikita ran over to help.

"How are you feeling, baby?" Nikita kissed Debare on the lips.

"Better, the meds they gave me knocked me out," smiled Debare looking down at his leg.

"You'll feel the pain when it wears off." Nikita smiled sitting down on a chair nearby.

"I guess I'll enjoy it, while it lasts."

"So who were those men after you last night, Nikita?"

"I don't know."

"You're not telling me the truth."

Nikita got up, turning her back. "Know your place, Peter."

"My life is now in danger, and I deserve to know what the fuck is going on."

"Those men were after something." Nikita turned back around. "It was a big mistake. I had something that should have stayed locked away."

"What was it, Nikita?" Debare acted as if he didn't already know.

She looked at him stupidly.

"Don't act like you didn't see it on my neck. You were looking at my breasts and ass all last evening."

"I think you're right about that," laughed Debare.

"The diamond. You stupid freak!"

"Is it real?"

"Of course, it is. It's one of the most prized diamonds on Earth. I know you heard of the Cullinan. Haven't you?"

"Oh shit!"

"I can't say anything else." Nikita walked over to the window, looking at the street. "They will come after me again." She turned back around to face Debare. "And I don't know when."

"So, what are you going to do?"

"I'll have to go into hiding."

Nikita was too young to defend herself. Debare could offer for her to stay at his place, but he was on a mission. He needed to find out where she got that diamond from and how deep her ties are with the Parliament.

"Frankly, I'm here to make you an offer." Her tone turned serious wasting no time. "I want you to be my personal bodyguard, Peter."

"Nikita, I'm not fit for the job."

Nikita came to his bedside and rubbed his face.

"Few would ever take a bullet for me, and you don't even know me." She said rubbing his chest with her tender white hands.

"Hire someone that's Russian."

"I trusted no one in my life until the other night." She started opening his shirt and moving her hands downwards.

"I will pay you a lot of money." Her head lowered to his cock, which was now bared.

"I-- I'm yours, under one condition," Debare

repeated as Nikita sucked and licked. "That I don't get killed."

"Believe me, our safety is my only priority, baby," whispered Nikita as she was enjoying pleasing the Nigerian. He leaned back and enjoyed Nikita snatching his soul.

Debare was discharged from the hospital after a week. Brian had secretly come by to see how Debare was doing. He debriefed Debare's story, telling him to rest, and focus on getting closer to Nikita. Brian didn't tell Debare he had someone else working on the mission; a British operative, Vlad who was half-Russian and British. He's been working with the Parliament for years as a government contractor in the oil sector. Vlad had very strong ties to the ministers and their families.

A taxi was called to pick up the Nigerian and take him to Nikita's. The fading sun's rays burned his skin when he got to the front entrance of the hospital. The Nigerian put on his sunglasses and limped to the taxi. The driver immediately took his bags and placed in the trunk.

As they drove through Moscow's neighbourhoods, Debare looked over his new messages. There was one from an unknown number that read, "I expect you -

Nikita." He smiled, knowing big brother was still watching him.

Twenty minutes later, the taxi halted at Nikita's. Debare was ready to pay but the driver told Debare it was covered. As the Nigerian got out of the car with the help of the driver, he checked out the surroundings. There were mansions with large gardens and the streets were clean. Debare put his bag and Brian texted him.

"Don't forget to turn on your phone's interpreter." The Nigerian rang the bell twice before Nikita answered through the intercom. Debare heard people laughing in the background.

"Good morning, mon amour?"

"Morning! It's Debare."

"Come in!" The gate then buzzed open.

There were colourful flowers on each side and the walkway's tiles were fancy. Loud music was coming from inside the house and there were guests walking around with drinks. As Debare made his way in, Nikita came out with two men looking stunning.

"Peter!" yelled Nikita holding a bottle of champagne. The men were looking strangely as the Nigerian approached.

"What's going on here?"

"Oh, I must've forgotten to tell you!" She said

placing the champagne on the table and embraced Debare. "I'm hosting tryouts today!"

"What kind of tryouts?"

"Oh, you'll see, mon amour. For now, drink some of this champagne with us. We are celebrating life!"

"I'm good."

Nikita went back inside where her guests were chatting and laughing at something one gentleman had said. Debare watched as they poured themselves drinks laughing and almost drunk. Nikita was pleased. Moments later, three young ladies had entered the garden, outfitted revealing tops. Debare put his hand over his mouth, wondering what is really going on.

"Your names and ages, please," Nikita spoke in English as she made sat.

"My name is Tanya, and I'm 21 years old." She was a tall slim girl with black hair. The young woman nodded looking at the next.

"I'm Sonya, I turned 24 yesterday." The young woman tucked a strand of hair behind her ear and smiled, placing her hands on her hips.

"Calina, I'm 23 years old." The last woman was so bashful that it made Nikita grin.

"Okay, girls tell me a little more." Nikita kept asking them questions and jotting down their answers.

At first, Debare thought Nikita was running a modelling agency. But was proven wrong when Nikita ordered the girls to remove their clothes. He sat entertained and didn't say a thing.

The girls were then ordered to play with themselves and had ten minutes to climax. Each was given toys and everyone in the room enjoyed their moans. Then, they were escorted to a room to get dressed. Nikita paid them and then went to the bathroom while telling everyone to take a break.

"Excuse me, by the way, what the hell does Nikita?" asked Debare standing next to two men smoking cigars.

One responded, "I guess she hasn't told you yet, huh?"

"I guess not."

Both men laughed and Debare tried but couldn't. The second man tried to cut him off his comrade from speaking but couldn't. "Our boss runs the largest prostitution ring in Russia. There will always be ladies around to fuck as long as you are employed."

Both men laughed loudly holding their hands over their mouths to suppress the noise. Debare realized he had been duped into working in the black market.

"It's weird she hasn't told you yet. I mean you're working for her after all. Am I correct?" said the second man in sunglasses while sipping and looking at the girls' CVs.

"Yeah, man. I knew that, but I was responsible for her gold deliveries and got transferred here today."

"Cool. Well, it's nice meeting you. What's your name?"

"Peter." Debare shook hands with the gentlemen and excused himself. Two minutes later, Nikita came back and Debare didn't wait for her to continue. He pulled her to the side and grabbed her firmly, "Are you running a prostitution ring?"

"Is there something wrong with that, mon amour?" Nikita freed herself from the Nigerian's grip.

"Yes, a lot."

"Listen, Peter. I don't have time for this right now. I'm working."

"I don't either, so be honest with me, why did you hire me?" Debare's voice grew louder.

"Because I felt sorry for you. Now, please don't make a scene in front of our special guests."

"I've been honest with you and almost got fucking killed. Now, you're the one deceiving me."

"Look, if you want to go, then go. Don't think I can't find a replacement for you."

"Fine, I'll stay. But don't get us killed with your foolishness?"

As Nikita was leaving, she grabbed the Nigerian by his cock in front of the guests and said, "I told you in the beginning, your job is to keep me safe. I'll deal with this black thing later this evening."

Debare went to the side, hiding his erection but checking out the remaining women who came for the next hour. After the girls and men walked out, Debare saw the couch was so wet that Nikita would have to throw it away. Nikita closed the front door, and came back to Debare, kissing him on the neck. Debare tried resisting and Nikita went down to her knees, opening the Nigerian's zipper.

Twenty minutes later, Nikita finished with Debare and left Debare in the room. The Nigerian assumed he could leave. As he was heading to the front gate, Nikita's guardsmen pointed their weapons at him and instructed him to go to the back. A guard pulled out a room key and handed it to the Nigerian. The Nigerian then saw Nikita come back and out.

"You will stay with me for at least half of the month and I'll be back this evening for more." Nikita went into the kitchen with two of her maids.

"Oh my God!" Debare groaned as the guards escorted him to his quarters.

Two weeks later and after loads of sex with Nikita, Debare finally got back home, seeing much hadn't changed. He thought Brian would have come by to clean it up, but there was no sign of anyone entering. Brian didn't even bother calling him after he left the hospital. Debare could not wait to talk to Brian which was quite strange.

The Nigerian threw his duffle bag on the couch and sat wondering what was going on back in Lagos with his shop and secretary. Brian told him he'd take care of it but he still felt sorry for Daraja.

He turned on the TV finding most of the channels in Russian. "Are there any fucking Africans on TV here?" sounded Debare. The BBC was the closest thing to Nigeria that he could find, so he turned up the volume.

"A foreign spy is being sought by Cheka, and we have leads in the case," said the Minister of Finance." Debare turned it off. "No more going out. I'm a wanted man. Shit, where the hell is Brian? " Debare dialled Brian's number and after ten rings he answered.

"Hello, Brian. What's up? The police are still on me. Get me the hell out of here."

"I told you before that's not my problem, I can't do anything about it, now."

"Muthafucker," muttered Debare.

"What did you say?"

"Man, they will kill me once they discover me. Abort this mission or whatever words you guys use."

Debare walked over to the balcony and looked outside to see if anyone was there.

"They don't have your ugly face, so they won't discover you. There are many refugees in the country that look just like you. All the black guys look the same, right?"

"You fucking cunt!"

"Cheer up dude and hey man, it's good you called after drowning in all that Russian pussy. Shit, look at it like you were on vacation.

"Yeah, right."

"Anyway, I need you to assist Austin tonight."

"Who's Austin?" My replacement?"

"Yes, and you need to be a lookout for him tonight. He has an important mission objective. Please don't get fucking caught."

Debare rolled his eyes. "Alright fine, where?"

"The Ball at Winter Palace. The ministers will be there and while they're smooching, Austin will go in and question Vlad. We got everything set up. All you have to do is stand by the door. It's a piece of cake."

"There's nothing easy working with you, guys. Anyway, isn't Vlad working for us?"

"Yes, but this guy is different. By the way, they sure look like fucking brothers. Anyway, Vlad is the one who found the Cullinans and is probably the middle man for the transactions. Your tape from the Senate

Building connects him but we still need more proof. Remember the Ball, 9 PM and don't be late."

Fifteen minutes before nine, Debare got dressed for the Ball. As he was leaving, he received a message: "Meet me at the back gate.—A.A." which stood for Agent Austin.

Debare giggled at his strange signature and locked his door. Believing his motorcycle was outside, he realised that he left it at the club. "Shit, I need to call a taxi."

Ten minutes late, Debare reached the Ball and went to the back entrance, noticing dozens of expensive cars parked. He lit up a cigarette, expecting Austin to show up on time but he didn't. Minutes later, a black van pulled up in front of the Nigerian and a white man hopped out. "Debare Balogun."

"Yes."

Austin buttoned up his suit jacket while offering his hand.

"Austin?"

"Right, your job is simple. Just do as I say. Understood?" Austin's cockiness annoyed Debare.

"Alright."

"We'll be waiters for tonight."

"Waiters? Brian told me--"

"Mission objectives have been refreshed."

"God damn! You guys work on the fly?"

"We don't. It's just part of the job. Now, get ready."

Austin pushed Debare forward and then pulled him back.

"Before we enter, you'll need this." Austin handed him an earpiece that could barely fit in his hands. Debare put it in as they walked through the cooking staff's section.

Austin greeted a worker and Debare nodded. The man whispered to Austin something. That man then leads them to another room to change from their tuxedos into waiter outfits.

Austin instructed Debare to serve drinks to the Ministers at Table B and do it slowly to eavesdrop. Some waiters in the area looked at Debare suspiciously, but Austin told them in Russian Debare was in-training and that he was the regional manager. They laughed at a joke Austin made to break the ice.

"I can't serve Boris," said Debare before they went inside the ballroom.

"Why not?"

"He'll recognize me."

"Fine, serve Alina and her daughter and I'll serve the rest."

Austin opened the doors and high-class officials

were accompanied by their spouses. Everyone was laughing and talking. A pianist at a white grand set the mood. Austin pointed at a corner in the room; 'Table B' was lit up by a red mini lamp. Alina was alongside with her youngest daughter, Tatiana who resembled Gala and another man.

"Don't leave my sight," warned Austin as he disappeared into the crowd.

"Champagne for Table B?"

Alina and her attendants looked the Nigerian strangely. Tatiana was first to take a glass and then Alina and the man followed, thanking Debare.

"Get us some snacks, please," Alina suddenly ordered.

"Right away" Debare nodded whispering, "Fucking brat!"

The Nigerian headed to the kitchen grabbing the first snack tray he spotted. "Where the fuck is Austin?" Debare looked in the crowd but couldn't find him.

When Debare returned, Alina and Gala were there chatting while the third was in the lobby taking a phone call. Tatiana grabbed a few pieces of chocolate.

"Is that all, madam?"

"That's all unless you can dance for me."

"No, ma'am. I'm sorry but I cannot. I'm on duty." Debare turned away, mumbling, "What a fucking racist!"

Alina put her hand over her mouth but soon apologised. Debare nodded walking off while hearing a beep in his earpiece. It was Austin.

"Debare?"

"Where are you?" whispered Debare trying to spot him in the crowd.

"Go to the second floor now!"

Debare rushed upstairs. "Which door?"

"The last on the right."

Austin was kneeling next to a drunken man. "This is Vlad, my friend. He discovered the diamonds. Now, he will be fucking famous."

"Yes, that's me—your friend and mine," slurred Vlad.

Debare closed the door. "What about Alina downstairs?" whispered Debare.

"What's the fucking—big secret?" blurted Vlad.

"We're projecting your movie. You'll be a star in Hollywood," replied Austin.

Austin resumed his conversation with Debare. "Boris and Alina have nothing to do with the discovery. Let us find out more," Austin giggled while handing a glass of wine to Vlad.

"Now, Vlad. How did you get the diamonds? My

director here needs to know. Anything you tell us, we'll put it in your blockbuster."

"The owner of the Popigai Crater gave them to me. He knew I had the widest range of transportation--" His words slurred. "That fucking dirtbag owes me a lot of money, so let's call it payback." Vlad drank until the wine spilled down on his shirt.

Debare started recording their conversation, got closer and drank along with them.

"You're a rich man. Why do you need these diamonds, anyway?"

"They're for our people, not me; Russia's poor but many of my comrades are greedy."

"This news will make a good plot; A Russian who discovers diamonds to give them back to the poor," said Austin.

They laughed while Vlad pointed for Debare and Austin to drink more.

"Where are the other two?" asked Debare. Austin didn't want the Nigerian to interfere.

"Alina and Boris have them. I guess. Those two are some greedy motherfuckers. By the way, what does "motherfucker" mean?" slurred Vlad.

"I honestly don't know. Do you, Debare?"

Debare shrugged.

"Interesting! Vlad, you said Alina has a diamond, but Boris wants to sell the other," said Austin.

"I think Alina sold hers," interrupted Debare.

"Shut up?" interjected Austin.

"What the fuck did you say? Alina--" said Vlad.

"Let's talk about that part one more time. Give us a minute, Vlad. Help yourself."

Debare pulled Austin to a separate room. "MI6 gave me a tracker to put on her phone. She had the diamond weeks ago but its whereabouts have gone cold."

"What about Boris?"

"I don't know." Debare shrugged pondering over the diamond Nikita had on her neck.

Austin then returned and said, "We have more than enough to get your movie started."

But Vlad was passed out.

"Let's get out of here, Debare."

They exited and went back through the kitchen to their starting point.

"I have everything I need. You are free to go," said Austin.

"Wait, what are we going to do now?"

"Nothing. I'm going on vacation. Brian will call you. My job is finished." Austin lit up a cigarette and minutes later, the black van pulled up again.

"Nice working with you. You cocky bastard."

"Hey fuck some chicks while you're out here."

"Sir, yes, sir."

Two weeks passed without much progress from MI6 and Debare was back at Nikita's. He crept inside her bedroom while she was in the shower. As Debare dug in her drawers, Nikita surprisingly came.

"What are you doing in here?" Nikita walked closer; she was covered in a towel and her head was still dripping wet.

"Organising your clothes. Man, your place is sloppy. I nearly tripped while coming in." The Nigerian closed the drawer before she noticed.

"My things are okay. You're not allowed in my personal space without permission. Remember, you're here to protect me, so go downstairs and stand by until I get ready." Just as Debare was leaving, Nikita's phone rang. She picked up as Debare reached the top of the steps.

"Boris, is our deal still on for tonight?"

"I don't know if I should bring the diamond. I almost got killed over it." Debare eavesdropped hoping to gather more. He leaned against the door hearing the words, "I miss you."

"This lady is just like her business," pondered Debare as Nikita kept talking.

Boris was married with young children. He looked like a piece of shit. "How could Nikita even fall for someone like that?" wondered Debare. As he tiptoed towards the steps, a vase flipped over from a mahogany stand.

"Wait, one second, sweetheart," said Nikita. Debare picked up the fragments and hurried down the steps. "Is that you, Matilda?"

Matilda, her housemaid, was downstairs and yelled back, "No." The old woman had the entire house smelling like pasta. Debare savored the smell and kept walking back and forth in the kitchen, looking inside. Matilda sensed his presence and offered him a small plate.

"Hmm, this almost tastes like Jollof."

The old woman smiled although it was clear she didn't understand English. Nikita came downstairs ten minutes later. Her hair was still wet, but she seemed mesmerized by the pasta.

"Debare, join me at the table, please."

"Tonight, I'm invited to a special engagement," spoke Nikita as Matilda set the table. "The venue will be packed with legislators, and I'll need you to guard me."

"What kind of special engagement, if you don't mind me asking?"

Nikita, while biting her food, presented the Nigerian a picture on her phone of a nude man. "It's an art expo celebrating Russian history."

"Anything else?"

"No, Debare."

"So, I guess there'll be a party afterward?"

"Yes, at Sky City."

Debare found out Nikita was meeting Boris at the Expo. He contacted Brian and his instructions were clear; gather intel only.

Nikita and Debare dined beforehand; gossiping away about life in Moscow and Nigeria. After an hour of Nikita getting dressed and some short fore-play, the two headed out. Debare drove, and neither of them spoke much while riding. Nikita sensed something.

"Is there something wrong, Peter?"

"No, why do you ask?"

"You're acting strange. May I shouldn't have played with you before we left?"

"No, it's okay. I'm just concentrating on tonight. That's all."

"I don't believe that. You sound like a jealous man."

"I'm not, Madame. We're almost there."

Minutes later, the Nigerian reached the Expo. He got out first, grabbing his earpiece and whispered, "Mic check." Brian responded, "All clear. Have fun!"

Nikita's dress was choking her in all the right places. Debare opened the car door for Nikita and watched her step out; fixing her dress and hair. As they went up hand in hand up the steps, the spotlight turned on her. The Expo was packed. "These ministers party so much, I wonder how they have time to help their people," pondered Debare.

"The diamond's in my handbag, Peter."

"Are you fucking crazy?" Debare grabbed her arm causing both to come to a stop.

"What is it now?

"We'll get killed over your foolishness?"

"That's why you're here, to protect me and you," Nikita said smiling.

"Alina!" Nikita yelled out excited, while Debare tried his best to conceal his face.

"Long time no see." Alina's voice was being picked up on the earpiece from afar.

"I missed you, how are the girls?"

"Oh, they're just lovely, we're sending off Daria to college this year."

Daria was the youngest of three siblings and the most polite.

"Send my hugs her way and tell her I wish her luck." Nikita hugged Alina goodbye.

Debare followed Nikita hoping Alina didn't recognize him. Boris was easy to spot. He and his wife were talking with a group of ministers. Nikita stopped.

"What's wrong?" asked Debare hearing Nikita curse Boris's wife under her breath.

"Hmm. Nothing."

Nikita then turned her attention to the exhibit's portraits. Throughout the night, Nikita was offered cocktails but Debare kindly refused anything sent her way.

After most began leaving, Boris saw Nikita telling her to meet him in the parking lot. Nikita told Debare to stay put but he didn't bother listening. He crept behind and hid behind a dumpster.

"The diamond, where is it, you stupid woman?" Boris screamed.

"I have it and why do you need it?"

"Excuse me? I need it, now. I don't have time for your childish games."

"Why? To give it to some other tramp?"

"Get your popcorn ready! Haha!," said Brian through the earpiece.

Boris slapped Nikita and the echo ricocheted through the parking lot. "How dare you, you fucking slut?"

She grabbed him. "You told me you would fucking divorce her! I believed you." Nikita began crying.

"Divorce my wife? For you, the head of the biggest prostitution ring in Moscow? Please." Boris laughed. "I would never divorce her for a low—life like you. But you know what we can do tomorrow morning on my way to work." Boris got close whispering something in her ear. Nikita pushed him away.

"You'll never get the diamond, you stupid bastard! I fucking hate you." Nikita slapped Boris and kicked him in the balls. Nikita then ran out the parking lot, crying. Debare couldn't stop laughing as Brian was ridiculing Nikita inside his earpiece. The Nigerian got back in time as Nikita neared him.

She was visibly agitated, wiping her tears. She told Debare to bring the car. When the Nigerian asked why she wasn't going to the afterparty, Nikita said she was tired.

The drive home was quiet, and Nikita told Debare to

take the car to his place for the night after letting her out.

Debare went home and when he arrived, he found the gate unlocked. Clutching his pistol, he crept inside. There were noises coming from the living room as he tiptoed. Brian saw his shadow and told him to put the gun down.

"You scared the shit out of me!" said Debare.

Austin was with him, watching TV and sipping on a beer.

"Why the fuck both of you are here anyway?"

"I have a spare key. Sometimes, I can't stay at home. My fucking girlfriend is getting on my nerves. These Russian girls just want to go out and party!" said Brian as Austin laughed.

"Anyway," replied Debare.

"I see you've been out working or working out?"

"Running errands, you mean."

"In a tux?"

"Art Expo. You heard the shit."

"Enough of the small talk. We need to debrief," said Brian.

"Ok, give me a minute to change."

Austin began speaking. "The fourth diamond is still missing."

"It's still missing? Shit! We don't have any intel on its location?" added Brian.

"No, we have to go over the clues we have so far," Austin sat up. "Alina sold hers and got two billion dollars. She's the richest fucking woman in Russia."

"There's nothing we can do now but I got a feeling that the last is with that dirtbag, Boris. He's the most dangerous; working for the Russian Mafia part-time."

"Part-time? Debare chuckled. "I've been on Nikita, but can't get close enough to verify if she has a real or fake one," added Debare.

"Let's assume it's real for now. Now back to Boris, MI6 found he's taking a business trip this weekend," added Austin.

"A business trip? Maybe he's going to sell the remaining diamond? With the Parliament's sessions wrapped up, it's the perfect cover," said Brian excitedly.

"Hey, Brian. My trails on Alina got cold and I need to get back to her before we lose her," suggested Austin.

Brian looked at Debare having second thoughts if the Nigerian should be the one trailing Boris. "I guess you have another job, kiddo."

"We'll be late, hurry!" Nikita rushed out, tossing Debare her luggage. They are traveling to Novorossiysk, 1,500 kilometres from Moscow. Boris invited Nikita on the business trip and Debare sensed it was a trap. The Nigerian started growing a beard and looked aged. From Boris' conversations before the trip, intel suggested he was going to get the diamond from Nikita, one way or the other.

After the flight, Debare and Nikita were driven to an exotic hotel called the Expromt, paid for by Boris. Nikita's suite was huge, and she raved about it. Before they coming downstairs, Debare and Nikita made out.

"Don't be upset if you see something between Boris and me, Peter. It's only business." She grabbed Debare's cock while the elevator descended. "I'll take care of this big ole thing later when I get back." She kissed Debare causing him to moan.

"No--No worries, Madam. I--I'm at your service," slurred the Nigerian.

The elevator doors opened to a ball in the lobby's terrace. Debare was close to her, looking serious as Nikita walked in. Everyone complimented her for her fancy attire.

"So where is he?" asked Debare.

Nikita looked around for Boris. "Let's get a drink." Minutes later, Boris arrived with his personal bodyguard. His eyes were fixed on Nikita and stepped right over.

"I see you finally made it."

"I wouldn't miss it for the world." Nikita smiled as Boris eyed her sexy figure. He kissed her on the cheek and then looked at Debare. "You are?"

"Peter, sir." Debare put his hand for Boris to shake.

"I see you found yourself a job." Boris mocked as Nikita appeared confused.

"Do you two know each other?"

"We met a few weeks ago at the refugee protest. You were the one who gave me my pen back. Right?"

"Yes, sir. It was me. Madame Nikita has been very gracious in giving me this job, sir."

"Enough of the small talk, let's have a good time. Nice seeing you again, Peter." Boris walked off with Nikita.

They spoke in a corner as Debare stood by Boris' bodyguard catching Nikita's chat through the earpiece.

"We are waiting for Grigor to come. He'll have the money," said Boris. Nikita was excited and it appears she was selling the diamond.

As nightfall descended, the reception area was congested, Debare got word that he had to stop the diamond from being sold. Boris and Nikita dipped out for an hour and Debare knew they were fucking. Once they returned, they came back to the gala briefly and then headed to the elevators. Debare put down his drink and followed them, dodging behind the wall corner. He tried getting closer as overheard they were getting ready to meet with Grigor.

"He's almost here," said Boris after closing his flip phone.

"Debare! Debare!" yelled Brian in his earpiece.

"Shut up!" Debare pulled the earpiece out.

Boris and Nikita were still at the elevator when Debare ran into them. Nikita turned around happy to see the Nigerian.

"Peter, come here."

"Yes, Madam?"

"You'll escort a man inside by the name of Grigor when he arrives. We'll be in Room 340." Nikita winked as they walked inside the elevator.

Debare nodded and went back to the lobby.

"I'm taking my break now," shouted the receptionist to the doorman.

"Ok," shouted the doorman back leaving him to do desk duty. Grigor arrived, standing outside the parking lot,. He was talking on his cellphone while smoking a cigarette.

"Think fast, Debare," whispered Debare to

himself. Debare looked around spotting no one. He went back to the elevator and then crept back to the desk. Once the Nigerian was behind him, he injected him with a syringe causing the doorman to fall to the ground asleep. He was snoring like a baby within seconds.

Debare carried him to a nearby closet and removed his hat and his nametag. The Nigerian came out to the front desk fixing himself as Grigor walked through the sliding doors looking around. He was wearing a tailor-made Italian suit.

"Good evening sir, may I help you with your luggage?"

Grigor smiled. "Oh, pardon me. I haven't used English for a long time. But thank you, I have nothing but a carryon," said Grigor looking towards the elevators.

"Have you checked-in online?"

"No, but I'm here to visit a few of my colleagues from work. Perhaps you can assist me?"

"The names, please." Debare moved away from the desk trying to hurry just in case the receptionist came back.

"Boris Petrov and Nikita Andreeva."

Debare looked noticing that Grigor wasn't alone. Four men in black leather jackets were standing outside, wearing sunglasses, looking around. Debare knew the men were after Grigor.

Debare motioned for Grigor to follow him to the elevator. The men in black came inside to the reception as the receptionist came back to greet them.

"How can I help you gentlemen this evening?" she said in Russian.

"Out of our way, you fucking bitch," one man pushed her on the ground as they ran to the elevators.

Debare and Grigor hurried inside and the doors closed. They heard the men loud voices and banging on the door as the elevator ascended.

"What's going on? Those men? Where are we going?

Debare told him he was taking him to Nikita and Boris. The elevator reached the last floor, and they got off. Luckily, there was only one elevator working.

"Where are Boris and Nikita?"

"Just down the hall, we're almost there." He pushed Grigor in front of him.

Debare grabbed his pistol and hit Grigor in the back of the head, causing him to faint. Then, he dragged him to a nearby closet. Moments later, Nikita called the Nigerian. "What's taking so fucking long?" she said screaming.

"Grigor's not here yet. I'm in the lobby," said Debare going to the maintenance lift on the other side.

"Check outside, maybe he's lost. Hurry up!"

"Okay. The connection is cutting out—." Debare hung up and pressed the down button. The doors suddenly opened and four men walked off, grabbing Debare.

"What do you think you're doing?" Debare tried fighting them off. The men said nothing as they blindfolded him and took him away.

The blindfold was removed and the men stood over the Nigerian wearing black masks. "Where the fuck am I?" Debare was seated while the men were looking at him.

"What the hell is going on here?"

"Shut the fuck up." Debare was slapped in the back of the head causing him to jerk.

Another person came in. He pulled off his mask and revealed his face.

"Brian!?" said Debare.

"How dare you, you fucking bloody traitor!" Brian's face was red as he slapped Debare across his face making his head jerk again. "How could you do this to me!? I trusted you for God's sake!"

"What did I do? What the hell, Brian?"

"What did you do, huh? You've been hiding intel."

"What are you talking about? I told you Nikita has a diamond and I don't know if it's real."

"You want it for yourself. Don't you?" Brian crossed his arms.

"No, I don't. I was trying to do the mission myself to show you I'm worthy."

Brian hiring Austin to replace him made Debare expendable. The Nigerian feared going to prison for life.

"You did nothing, fucking nothing!" said Brian tossing the books on the table. "If you wanted to tell us the truth, you would've done it from the beginning. You despicable piece of shit. Did you think I wouldn't find out, stupid fuck? You can't hide anything from me." Debare hoped the earth would open and swallow him first before hearing Brian's taunts.

"Is Boris with her?"

Debare didn't answer thinking if he told Brian that they would kill Nikita.

"Boris is smarter than we think. They probably already left," said Brian prancing the room with three other agents.

"Answer me, you fucking prick!" Brian punched Debare in the face.

"Yes, yes. "

"What fucking room?"

"Room 340."

"What are you waiting for? Go now!" Brian ordered his men and turned back to Debare. "I swear I'll make your life a living hell from now on. I have the fucking power to wipe you off the face of this Earth with a snap of my finger. You hear me?" Brian turned away from Debare and took a phone call from central command. Debare didn't move; shocked.

"How long has the affair been going on between Nikita and Boris?"

"I don't know."

"Her fucking boy-toy bodyguard doesn't know? Get the fuck out of here!"

"I don't know honestly."

"Spare me your ignorance, please."

"They are a thing, that's all I know."

Brian didn't reply back looking at Debare's face, disgusted.

Ten minutes passed since Brian's men left. The group stormed in, panicking.

"Sir, there's no one there." said the leader. Brian turned to Debare, "Where are they heading or I will kill you right now?"

"I don't know. They were meeting Grigor. That's all I know."

"Search the fucking hotel from top to bottom." "As for you, you will find Nikita and that diamond, you clumsy fuck."

CHAPTER SIXTEEN

THE SAGA with Brian appeared to have no end. Now, Brian's agents were in and out of Debare's flat monitoring him and any communications on the feeds. There was an awkward silence while the agents were working and Debare was told to stay away. Meanwhile, MI6 had no clue on where Boris and Nikita had gone.

The Nigerian frustrated with Brian's orders broke his phone. Three days later, he received another by DHL. Brian told him if he had one more fuckup, he would be sent back to Nigeria. When the Nigerian put his Sim card in, a message popped up from Nikita.

"You disappeared out of nowhere, sweetheart. I'm home but not staying long. I'll see you soon – Nikita."

Brian came a few minutes later. "Hey, I heard you received a package? Where is it?"

Debare was clutching the phone in his hand and

Brian took it from him. "What do we have here?" Brian's smile faded as he read the message.

"She's in Moscow? Quick, get to her house now!" Brian rushed Debare pushing him towards the door. The agents got up as well logging out their laptops. "Check her fucking house up and down. "Take this tracker with you. Don't fuck this up, boy."

Brian didn't trust Debare to go by himself, so he sent Austin to trail him. Austin was waiting out front and they drove to Nikita's. The gate was locked, and the keypad was shut off. Matilda heard knocking on the door and came. When she saw Debare, she waved. She let the Nigerian and Austin inside and showed them to the living room.

"Nikita was here two hours ago. I don't know why she left suddenly," said Matilda saddened. Austin translated and tried comforting her. "It's fine, I'm sure she'll come back soon." Austin said in Russian nudging Debare to go on and speak.

"Listen, Matilda, Nikita forgot something and told me to take it from her room if that's not a problem." The Nigerian caressed her shoulder and the old woman smiled. "Go ahead, but please don't make a mess, Peter."

The room was straighten up apart from Nikita's closet. Her outfits were tossed everywhere, and the safe was left open.

"Fuck," snapped Austin. "Brian's going to kill us."

Debare told him to check every drawer whilst he checked under the mattress. Austin pulled out boxes of jewellery, but there was nothing but cheap gold necklaces inside. "The diamond's gone." Austin stopped, placing his hands on top of his head.

"What do we do now?" Austin told Debare to stop searching for the moment.

"Think Debare! Think! Where could have she hid it?"

"She never let me even come close to that thing. I know we need to hurry!"

They went downstairs, seeing Matilda cleaning the living room. "Matilda, did Nikita leave anything for me?"

"Oh yes, I forgot. There's an envelope. I don't know what's inside."

"Can you bring it?"

"It's in her office on the table down the hall."

Debare led the way while Austin stormed inside. The envelope was there and Austin grabbed it and tried ripping it open. Debare snatched it away. "It's mine." The Nigerian pulled out a stack of American hundred dollar bills, with a note saying: "Sorry, I wasn't able to pay you for your services. Perhaps we'll meet again."

"Nikita's gone forever," said Debare.

"Matilda!" Austin yelled. Matilda ran to the room stopping at the door with the duster in her hand. "Yes!"

"Do you have any idea where Nikita might've gone?"

"I don't know. That girl goes anywhere her feet will carry her."

"Just anything," pleaded Austin.

"I've known Nikita since she was a little girl. She was never like this until she became--." Matilda sat down holding her head.

"She's like my little girl. Her parents were always away and I was the one who basically took care of her." Matilda stated wiping away her tears.

Austin continued asking questions, but Matilda didn't want to say anything that would jeopardise Nikita's life. "Matilda, thank you for your time. I think we need to get going." Austin pulled on Debare.

As they were leaving, Debare's phone buzzed. A text message came in from Brian: "Go to the Parliament now, Alina's being arrested."

Debare showed it to Austin and he said: "Let's go!"

"I wonder why the police are arresting her," said Debare while Austin was driving.

"While you were busy attending to Nikita's

fancies, Brian pulled a fast one." Once they arrived, Debare jumped out first. The street was swarmed with news vans and many people on the scene.

"Stop! You have no right to do this!" yelled Alina as she was being taken away, handcuffed.

Police and military personnel were in front of the Parliament building guarding as the other Ministers watched in shock. Debare looked over at Austin who was chuckling.

"What now?" asked Debare.

"We must find Nikita and Boris."

Alina's attorneys took a position to answer questions about allegations. Shortly after it was over, Austin and Debare left. There was an unmarked car parked in the front. Debare opened the door finding Brian seated and another man standing above him.

"Brian?"

The man turned around. It was Vlad, the lead behind the Cullinan search.

"You must be Debare?" Vlad stood up to shake the Nigerian's hand.

"Yes, sir." Debare dodged looking at him.

Vlad was wearing a fancy suit and had an expensive-looking suitcase beside the couch.

"I heard a lot about you, son."

"Oh, yeah! I hope good things." Debare looked over to Brian.

"I'm Austin, sir," said Austin butting in. Vlad shook his hand and then sat. "Gentleman, we have work to do. Please sit down."

"Sadly, we have no new leads on the whereabouts of Nikita and Boris." Brian looked disgusted.

"They've probably have left Russia by now, but our intelligence is not 100% certain." Vlad began digging through his suitcase. "Let's not assume they haven't. I believe we need to break up our operations in search parties."

Debare wasn't paying attention and Brian kicked his leg under the table. Vlad chuckled knowing. "We'll find them. Everyone knows their profiles. Interpol has been alerted and we need the CCTV coverage at the borders for the last 24 hours." Vlad's laptop was being powered on as he spoke.

"That wouldn't be an issue. We have access to them," interrupted Brian.

"I don't think they left Russia yet. Austin and I just spoke to her maid, Matilda who said she was at the house a few hours ago," claimed Debare.

"Maybe she was lying," interrupted Austin.

"I planted a tracker on Boris' bag on my first assignment. If it's still working, maybe we can track him," replied Debare.

"I doubt he'd carry that bag around. Someone

would probably easily recognise him," said Vlad. "Sometimes, we find the trackers on dogs and cats."

Everyone laughed especially Debare who was the loudest.

"Seriously, knock it off. We can't sure, anyway. Let's break up this party and start with the CCTVs," commanded Vlad.

"I'll coordinate my men in the eastern region to begin accessing them," said Austin.

"I'll telelink the feeds through our cables back in the UK," added Brian.

"Tonight, we'll regroup. Time's not on our side, gentlemen. Let's go."

Vlad grabbed his laptop and other equipment and left while Austin went in a different direction. Debare was instructed to keep tabs on Nikita's house. He took the Metro to stay close in hopes she'd come back. The Nigerian went to a nearby cafe which was filled with cigarette and cigar smoke. It was almost impossible for Debare to find a spot to set up in peace.

While browsing through his phone, it rang. The call was from an unknown number.

"Hello?"

"It's me, Matilda. Meet me at the Red Square in 20 minutes."

"You speak English—?" Before his sentence ended, the phone hung up.

Debare looked up the location and saw he wasn't far from Red Square.

"Next stop: Red Square."

People were there taking snapshots and admiring the spectacle. There were many tourists, mainly from China. Debare waited in the cold, blowing his hands hoping Matilda would come quickly.

Minutes later, the old woman came up from behind the Nigerian. "Come, let's sit down somewhere." Debare walked behind her to a nearby coffee shop inside a plaza. Matilda ordered a cup of tea and Debare declined.

"I don't trust that Austin boy, so I need this to tell you alone. Nikita's still in Moscow."

"Where?"

The waiter came and Matilda paid him.

"I'm not sure, but I think she's at one of her old flats that are up for sale," said Matilda sipping.

"Do you know where?"

"I have a few mailing addresses, but I'm not sure if they are actually the places. She never told me where."

"You've been a great help. I'm trying to stop her from getting killed. These men are dangerous. Do you know if Boris is still with her?"

"I believe so. Yesterday, his wife called our house screaming. The crazy woman found out about him and Nikita."

"Why is Nikita so in love with that ugly guy anyway?"

"She's never been in love. Her father was never around when she was younger. He was always working abroad. When Boris met Nikita, she viewed him as a father figure. He took advantage of her childishness and she fell for his charm. You know what I'm saying?"

Debare laughed. "I know exactly what you are saying."

"Nikita and Boris met about years ago. I remember when he first came to the house. They carried in bottles of expensive wine every time he visited and spent a few nights a week together." Matilda looked down at one spot as she spoke. "It was the first time I ever saw my little Nikita smile so much." Matilda's hands then began shaking. "Now, she runs off with this crazy man. I never like him personally. Nikita gave her heart to this ugly ass motherfucker."

They laughed and Debare held her hands.

Matilda excused herself. Debare hugged her and promised he'd find and protect Nikita. The Nigerian looked at the mailing addresses and hurried out to begin searching. Debare had a few hours left before meeting back with Brian, Austin, and Vlad at his flat.

The Metro ride was short and the Nigerian checked the first mailing address on his GPS. Debare pondered why Nikita would buy property in such a ravaged neighbourhood.

Once he reached the place, he headed up to the seventh floor. The building appeared to only have a few tenants. "Apartment 57." He pulled out a set of tweezers and had picked the lock.

The place was small and Nikita was nowhere to be found. The Nigerian closed the door and went back to the Metro. The second location was only three blocks from the station in a better area. There were wealthy people residing there and it would be harder to get in. After the Nigerian told the security guard of his relationship with Nikita, he let him in. But, she wasn't there either.

It was almost nine at night, and Debare was smoking inside the parking lot of his home. When he opened his door, Vlad, Austin, and Brian were already inside.

"Did you come up with anything?" asked Brian.

"Matilda gave me addresses of two apartments, but Nikita wasn't there."

"We'll never find them!" Vlad said angrily. He stood up and walked over to the balcony.

"We didn't find anything on the CCTVs, so they must still be in the country," said Austin.

Austin turned on the TV and saw something. "Hey shut up."

"Please return our father to us! We'll pay anything!" said Boris' daughters assuming someone kidnapped their father.

"What the fuck is this?" yelled Brian.

"Sounds like the world believes someone kidnapped Boris," said Vlad not surprised. The news conference ended with a commercial break.

"Debare, quick give me the IP address of Boris' tracker," commanded Brian. Debare took out his phone and kept scrolling through the codes. He gave it to Brian who gave it to Vlad. For minutes, the room was in suspense as Vlad kept punching keys on his laptop.

"Gentleman, we have a fucking location."

"Yes!" shouted Debare, pumping his fist in the air.

CHAPTER SEVENTEEN_

"WE'RE GOING to St. Petersburg, fellas, so bundle up. It's colder than a motherfucker out there. Meet back in thirty," Vlad ordered Brian, Austin, and Debare and a small contingent of agents.

Within an hour, everyone was onboard Vlad's black van heading through a bad snowstorm for a 9-hour drive to St. Petersburg. Brian was given instructions to do whatever to get the diamond even if it costed lives. The team's weapons were locked and loaded. Boris was identified as target #1 and Nikita #2. No one knew how this will end. Thoughts raced through Debare's mind as they were given preparations from Vlad and Brian.

The snowstorm was so awful that flights in and out of Moscow had been cancelled. Vlad in the meantime hacked Nikita's IWatch after discovering the tracking device in Boris's suitcase suddenly stopped sending signals.

"Apartment 10B. Dernov Apartment House. I've got them." screamed Vlad. "Maybe Nikita is making love with the watch on. There's a bunch of movements."

Everybody laughed.

The overall plan was for the Nigerian to first persuade Nikita to surrender before the Russian forces got to them and executed them in cold blood.

Brian warned Debare that if he fucked up, he wouldn't hesitate to execute Debare himself and the mission would be ended. Debare laughed at Brian, but Brian was serious.

"How far away are we?" asked Austin, seated next to the driver.

"About fifteen minutes away, sir."

Brian continued looking out the window while talking on the satellite phone with Robert, the division chief of MI6 in London. Brian kept reassuring him the mission would be a success.

The countrymen as they drove by appeared to live in simplicity while the marketplaces were crowded with merchants and farm animals. The scenery reminded Debare of markets back home. After this experience, he promised himself to never cheat a customer ever again.

The black van made a sharp turn and then stopped on an empty street a few blocks away from St. Petersburg's central market.

"This is your stop, Debare. Check your earpiece to see if it's on. Pay attention to every detail we've gone over and don't mess up." Brian patted him on the back.

Debare gave the team a thumbs up. This was his sovereign chance, and the Nigerian knew it.

The van pulled off, and they left the operation in Debare's hands. The unit went on standby as each team member exited a few blocks apart, disguised as locals strolling. Debare walked until he reached the parking area of an 18th-century Victorian building. A security guard met Debare with his hand on his old gun. "How can I help you?" the guard responded in English seeing Debare. The man's old wrinkly face showed he'd been working this same job for most of his life.

"I forgot my keys inside the condo. I just moved in yesterday," chuckled Debare. The guard wasn't amused.

"I don't remember seeing your face around here. When did you move in?"

"The other guard - he was fat - came to help me up with my stuff two nights ago."

"Oleg's helping someone out? That's a first." The old man laughed and told Debare to come inside.

The Nigerian shook his hand and took the stairs. He readied himself as he came closer to the suite. Making his eyes watery, the Nigerian tapped on the door of Apartment 1oB. Waiting for what seemed like ages, Nikita opened the door wearing a sheer bodysuit.

"Nikita! Oh, Baby! I missed you." Debare's tears dropped as he embraced her. Nikita's hair was cut short and dyed brown.

"Peter?" said Nikita looking puzzled.

"Do you know how hard it was to find you, my love?"

"Come inside. I was just cleaning up." Nikita led him to the living room.

"Where were you? God, you'll get yourself killed. I got the envelope from Matilda," said Debare taking a seat.

"I've been busy with my businesses. I needed a break away from home." Nikita sat across from Debare. Vlad was trying to get through the Nigerian's earpiece but there was static.

"What the fuck? Not now," murmured Debare.

"Debare, can you hear me? The men are almost

near your location. Keep her busy." Vlad's voice kept interrupting Debare's attention.

"Nice." Debare slurred his words; partly responding to Nikita but signalling to Vlad, okay.

"So, how did you find me?"

"Matilda told me to help you get out of this mess. She gave me a few addresses but still, I couldn't find you. There was a broadcast on TV claiming that Boris had been kidnapped."

Nikita looked at Debare unconvinced.

"Matilda, of course." Nikita gazed at her nails.

"She cares for you, Nikita and I do, too. I'm grateful for this job and I take it seriously."

"I see. So, she told you one of my secrets. How's she doing?" Nikita changed her facial expression.

"She's okay but sad because you're not around. She calls you her little girl."

"I am that for sure."

"Debare! Debare! Are you there? The connection's kept giving static. Is Nikita with you? We're waiting for you," said Brian.

"Now, Peter. You must be thirsty. I see you're sweating. Care for a drink?" She got up waiting not waiting for Debare to reply.

"Sure and fuck the shit out of her while we come there. We're minutes away," joked Vlad in the earpiece. "Tell her you to need to go to the bathroom and run the sink. Our thermal indicators have spotted the diamond inside the safe. Get to her room. I'm working on hacking it open for you right now!"

Debare was about to get up when Nikita came out of the kitchen with two glasses. "Here you go, my love." She stared at him. Debare took the glass and took a small sip. She came next to him and put her legs on top of his. Debare pushed her away gently.

"What's wrong, baby?"

"Nothing. I have to use the bathroom."

"Ok, take another sip first before you leave me. This is the best wine Russia has to offer. I'll take care of that big black thing when you come back."

Her words began slurring in Debare's mind as he took a few more sips. She lifted her glass in unison as the Nigerian went down the hallway. Debare noticed her room was next to the bathroom. He turned on the water and gathered himself. A minute later, he crept out into Nikita's room and forgot to close the bathroom door. There was a big trunk on top of her drawers. He opened it, going through everything inside; finding only necklaces and rings. Debare then got on his knees passing through each drawer but there was no diamond.

"Debare, are you inside? We are having a hard time getting in. The guard isn't at his post. Do you copy?" said Brian through the earpiece.

"Maybe he's on break. Hurry the fuck up! I don't see a safe here," whispered Debare.

As the Nigerian stood up, he noticed someone in the mirror. It was Nikita holding the Cullinan diamond in one hand and a gun in the other. "Looking for this?"

He turned around slowly facing her. "Yes, actually but it's not what you see."

"Save it, you treacherous fool! You're a bad man. I've trusted you and twice you have betrayed me. Guess what—" Nikita's words began slurring again and Debare's eyesight started blearing. Quickly, he was losing his senses and began kneeling.

"What have you done? I'm here to save you. You don't understand."

"Did you think you and your agents were going to get my diamond?"

The Nigerian felt a sharp pain in his heart and realised Nikita had poisoned him.

"Call a fucking ambulance. I don't want to die. I have a mother who needs me."

"Don't we all, Peter? I gave you something that would put you to sleep for a little while."

Debare's heart rate was irregular; slowing down as blood rushed to his brain. "Brian, come now, please! She poisoned me," said Debare.

"We're inside, kiddo. We're coming!" yelled Brian in the earpiece.

"May we see each other again--in the next life," said Nikita staring at Debare's pale face. She bent over and kissed his forehead as Debare's heart had stopped.

His body laid lifeless on the floor. Nikita went to pick up the earpiece which fell out Debare's ear. "You killed this good man, you fucking Americans."

"You fucking bitch. I will—" replied Brian.

Nikita stomped the earpiece to pieces and quickly gathered her things and left.

"Debare, Debare!" yelled Brian and Vlad. "Abort mission. Abort mission," yelled Brian and Vlad to the agents in their earpieces. They were already inside as they were making their way upstairs.

Nikita's obsession with the Cullinan diamond was more than her love for her own self. Its beauty mesmerised her and she'd do anything to protect it. She received intel from the Kremlin hours earlier and killed Boris by electrocuting him in her bathtub minutes before Debare arrived. Debare didn't see the body which was behind the shower curtains.

As the sole owner of the last Cullinan diamond,

Nikita became Russia's most powerful woman. She never wed and returned to her maid, Matilda who asked her about Peter's whereabouts. Nikita replied that he'd gone back to Nigeria because his mother was ill. Matilda knew she was lying but remained loyal until her death only a week later. Nikita had to tie up loose ends and Matilda's treasonable offense made her expendable.

Two weeks passed since Debare's death and his family in Nigeria kept coming to the shop asking Daraja about his whereabouts. She said told them he was away in China growing the business. It was a lie Brian told her when he paid the rent and her salary every month. As long as her money was there, Daraja didn't ask any questions.

Vlad stayed behind in Russia while Austin and Brian went back to the UK. The BBC later interviewed MI6 after a WikiLeaks revelation tied them to the Nigerian's death. MI6 denied the allegations and said it was fake news.

Although they publicly denied the report, MI6 regularly remembered Debare as the Nigerian who lost his life. Brian and Austin spoke of him often as they drank after work, always tipping their glasses to the Nigerian who gave his life for the cost of his freedom.

JASON SMITH

When one talked about survival, the first thing that come into the minds of the people was surviving in a forest, in a mountainous region, or at sea. But what most didn't expect was that survival, in truth, meant the ability for one to live in such situations that no one else could ever consider or hope of being in. Survival, in a nutshell, means that someone lived in a place without the natural resources that one would find in a comfortable house or a comfortable home. That is what it meant to survive. And that is what the young boy by the name of Jason Smith did.

Jason was merely sixteen and didn't think of himself as anyone special. He was just a simple boy with some a few friends living in a simple house without a worry in the world. Sure, he'd cry with everyone when someone inside of his family died and he'd laugh with everyone when there was a time to laugh, but he would not shed a single tear or give a single glance if someone suddenly jumped up and screamed that there was an outbreak of dancing monkeys in some random city, for it most certainly didn't concern him at all.

But when things went down a certain way, and when things didn't go his way, there was nothing he could do except for pray, pray that there was someone or something that would perhaps save him.

'*Please give me strength.*' He thought as he took deep breaths. '*Please give me strength. Please give me strength.*'

And the reason why he was doing such a thing was that he was currently tied over on the chair, alone, inside of a dark room with nowhere to go. He didn't know what he had to do, but he knew that if he didn't have the strength, then no one could save him and he'd definitely be alone in this world of complete and utter pain and agony. Yes, that was the case, he just couldn't do things all by himself.

His hands and legs were bound by some dirty rags that Jason couldn't believe were still in use. He could smell the dirty and disgusting pieces of filth still inside of the rags, and he could still smell whatever it was previously used for. He knew for a fact that if the rag was used against his mouth and his nose, he would pass out, but they were at least merciful enough to leave his face uncovered, yet put a simple ball-gag inside of his mouth. He knew that he was in a rock and a hard place and if he didn't do something, he was, for sure, going to die. But first, he needed to know where he was, why he was kidnapped, and who in their right minds would kidnap someone as destructive and as useless as him. Right, there was utterly no one that would give a care about him, no one, and that was what was making him cry out in utter pain and agony.

And in that moment of weakness, he realized something. He realized the words of his Grandfather, his dear old Grandfather who always told him every-thing he needed to know. His dear old Grandfather who always wanted him to be strong. Jason knew that his Grandfather was dead and he was not going to be able to see him succeed anymore, but he had left behind a very, very important lesson.

'Never be dependent on Someone, my Grandson. Never.'

That was his lesson. His Grandfather always wanted him to be an independent man and grow up to be perhaps the greatest of all the men that were out there, that was the only way that he could be great, the only way that he could be perfect. 'And always remain strong. Because if you aren't strong, then no one will be strong for you.'

Those were his words, and to this date, those were the words that Jason had followed. He was a simple boy, but he was a simple, independent boy. He didn't need his mother to sing him to sleep at night, he didn't need lights to sleep at night and he for sure didn't need anyone beside him, giving him the support that anyone else would need to live on and to survive, for that is how he had grown up to be strong and powerful.

'Alright, Jason, calm down. No god is going to listen to you if you cry out here like this, no god.' Jason thought as he slowly calmed down and controlled his breathing. He didn't want to be cooped up here like this, and he didn't want to stay here just because he couldn't do something to get out. He needed to get out and return home to his family and friends. He needed to get out of here or nothing was going to happen to him. 'Let's think, think, think. Alright, the guys are going to come behind me if I escape, so I have to be smart about things. I know that there are three males out here, and for me to escape, I need to cut through these rags. Thankfully, the best thing that I can do here is to actually think about these things properly.'

Shaking his head and appearing to be in control over himself, Jason grinned. He knew that they should have cut his overgrown nails, he just knew it. If they had done that, then it wouldn't have come to this, ever. His nails were large enough for him to actually chip off slightly, and sure they hurt, but after some time, he was able to actually make a nice, small cut in the rag. He knew that this wasn't supposed to be happening, but either these kidnappers were really desperate for the money, or they were out of supplies. The only problem was going to be the door, which was locked. And for him to escape out of the door, he would need for them to actually come in first. But if he took one out, then the other two would be behind him as well.

'Alright. First order of business, get to know your surroundings well,' the boy thought. He had to get out of here and then find a way to know where he was kept. And for that, he just had to wait for the right time. It would be a delicate process but he would have to be really smart about this, and for that to happen, he needed to be silent and sneaky. He praised his luck that he managed to get his hands and legs free by using his chipped off thumbnails and then picked up the rags and tied himself up properly again, this time, in a way that he could actually use his hands and legs.

And he knew that this was the perfect time because it was dinner time.

"Well, kiddo, it seems that luck is with you today. We've got some leftover pizza." The fat, smelly, disgusting oaf of a warden came into the room. He was smelling as bad as the rags and he was looking as disgusting as the status of the room itself. And this was the man that he was going to strike, one way or the other. He wanted the man to just pass out, someway, somehow. He wanted that to happen and he was going to make that a reality. And right now, he just had to think properly, just think about things and he would succeed. "Alright, where do I begin? Open your mouth."

But Jason stopped before he could begin. He knew that he would need the energy, and as bad as the pizza looked, he would still have to eat it somehow. So, he opened his mouth and let the man feed him the disgusting looking Pizza. And he almost made a face when the cold and obviously rotten taste of meat touched his tongue. He had a plan for this as well. He would stick the rotten pieces of meat to the side of his mouth and only eat the bread and the cheese, and after that was done, he would try to spit them out on a later date. As he ate the Pizza, Jason noticed that the door was left open and that was his chance.

As the last piece went into his mouth, Jason twitched his legs so he could use them. He simply swiped down off to the side of the man and grinned as the large, heavy-set man fell down to the ground in a large cry. He couldn't believe how big of an idiot this man was. Ripping apart the rags that he had purposefully tied so he could get up, he grabbed the plate and slammed it right on the man's head so hard that the man could barely see straight. Another slam was enough to knock him out in a deep sleep. Then he waited. For 10 full seconds, he waited, and since no one came, he just kept the tray with him, a nice, hard, metallic tray, and spat the rotten pieces of meat out on the man. Grinning widely, Jason merrily went on his way, ignoring everything else.

Getting out of the room was easy enough. He knew that there was someone out there waiting for the fat man to come back again, and he wasn't going to take any chances. He had to be smart about things, and strong as well. The only way he was going to succeed was by being smart. And smart he was.

He had to learn, he had to improvise and he had to observe. He could hear some rummaging in the area right beside the main room and the sound of the TV in the main room. So, that meant there were only two other people, he knew it. The first one was in the kitchen and the second one inside the main room.

So, he would go up against the one in the kitchen first, and then the one in the living room. That was the only way that this could work and the only way that this would be normal. The only way that this could go wrong right now would be if he made a mistake, and Jason didn't like mistakes at all. Nope, he did not. So, that is why he became even sneakier than he already was. He became the sneakiest that he could be and was slowly sneaking down to the ground floor of the house that he was in, and directly to the kitchen.

This guy was not fat and slender. But he was short and was definitely not knowing of him. Walking closer to him, he slammed the tray hard on the man's head, and Jason watched as the man came toppling down. He ran towards the edge of the door that led to the main room and waited at the side to see if someone would come in. Luckily, no one did, the voice of the TV was too loud for the third and probably the last person that was to know that something was horribly wrong.

He walked sneakily inside of the living room, looking up at the TV to find out what his location was. The first thing he saw was the slight snow outside in the tropical rainforest-like area. So, he was up north. Then he noticed the slightest difference between the actress and the News Channel that was on. It was a weather forecast. So, that would mean he was in CANADA!

'Alright. I am in Canada, what now?' Jason thought as he walked closer to the back of the couch. Another hard slam later, the third and the final guy was also knocked unconscious. Now was the start of the timer. According to him, he had three hours to get as far away from this place as he could. And that was not considering what else was out there. So, he had to run, and as fast as he could run at that. And he was going to run. But first, some supplies. Luckily, he was right beside the kitchen and there was some fresh food, water, and some weapons that he could use. Sure, it was a slight popper that he didn't have any guns, but he at least had knives, some canned survival food, and a radio of sorts. Even if he could give out a signal to someone, he had to know what was going on. He just had to.

And so, Jason Smith, after 10 full days of captivity in a shack in presumably Canada, got away from his captors.

CHAPTER TWO_

J ASON RAN.

Jason wasn't sure how long he had been running for when the wolves noticed there had been a person, but he could hear them barking to one another when they began to follow him. Jason knew he could never outrun them. (The wolf runs on average 42-60 miles per hour. It's been known to track its prey for days on end. It rarely needs more than a few minutes, though). He needed to do something, or he would die.

A tree.

His parents always had terrible trouble grounding him. The main problem was due to the tree that was outside his window. Jason hated being trapped inside and took every chance to escape by climbing up and down that tree. He had become incredibly good at climbing because of this. It had gotten so bad that his parents put an alarm on his window that went off whenever he opened it.

The alarm had been magnetic. Jason would always just take a magnet off the kitchen fridge and stick it on the alarm so that the device wouldn't realize the connection had been interrupted. It didn't stop him from sneaking out. His parents never figured it out.

Jason saw a tree large enough about fifteen feet ahead of him. The branches were out of his reach but that wasn't a problem. He kicked off the truck and shot up his hands to grab the lowest branch. Moving quickly, he swung up his legs and started to climb. Just in the nick of time, too. The wolves arrived just as he began to climb, and Jason felt the breeze of their snapping jaws as they tried to bite him and the scurrying of their claws as they tried to get up to the top of the tree.

Jason didn't look down. He didn't stop climbing. He just kept moving until the branches got so thin that they risked snapping. Finally, he stopped. Leaning against the trunk as he caught his breath, he looked down at the ground below.

The wolves were still there.

They were snarling and pacing below the tree, their claws still bloody from the mauling of some poor animal, or human. Then, the largest wolf leaped towards the tree. Its claws dug into the bark and held. It was climbing the tree.

Jason pressed against the tree in fear. He had to tightly cover his mouth with his hands to keep from screaming. He had been wrong. The tree wouldn't save him; it just made it harder for them to get to him. But he had trapped himself in the process. He couldn't climb anymore; the branches would snap if he went up and he'd pass right by the wolf if he went down. He couldn't jump to the ground, it was too high and there were still three wolves at the bottom. He closed his eyes and prayed to any deity that may be listening to save him. A crashing sound answered him.

The wolf was on the ground again, even angrier than it had been before. It was limping slightly on one foot, snarling and barking at its companions. The deep gouges in the tree answered Jason's unspoken question. It had fallen.

The wolves stayed for several more minutes before leaving. Jason waited with bated breath for any sign of them before beginning the trip back down the tree. Carefully, he placed his foot on a branch.

It snapped under his weight, and the branch fell to the ground with a dull thud.

The wolves swarmed out of their hiding place. Scrambling to pull himself back up, Jason beat a hasty retreat up the tree. The wolves had actually waited to see what he would do. They were so much smarter than he had thought. Than anyone had thought. And that scared him more than anything else that had happened that day.

It rained that night.

Tropical storms tended to come out of nowhere and leave just as quickly as they came. But while they were there, they were fierce, howling things that battered you with rain and wind until all you could do was cling, shivering to yourself as you waited for it to pass. It was in that manner that Jason spent the night.

The only good outcome of the storm was that it drove the wolves away. He had seen them disappear into the trees, illuminated by flashes of lightning.

'They must be returning to their den', Jason thought. 'Or they could just be sitting aside to see what I would do.' chimed in his pessimistic side. Before leaving the tree, he broke off branches and threw them to the ground in hopes of causing any waiting wolves to reveal themselves. None came, but Jason feared that was because they had learned to wait before pouncing.

Still, he couldn't spend the rest of his (quite possibly very short) life in a tree. Cautiously, he moved down the branches and hopped the remaining distance to the ground.

A bush rattled. His heart stopped. A small snake slithered out of the foliage and Jason sighed in relief. While turning to leave the area, he saw it. A large sickle claw was lodged into the bark of the tree. The wolf had been limping, Jason remembered. At the time, he had thought it was due to the fall, but apparently, it had lost a claw in the process, causing the limp. The claw still had some blood on it.

With an amazingly steady hand, Jason reached up and yanked it out of the wood. He stumbled backward with the force of it, but he had achieved his goal. The claw was now resting in the palm of his hand, just as wicked sharp and deadly as it had been the day before.

Wiping it on his pant leg, Jason realized that the claw could be incredibly useful to him. It could be used as a weapon while he was on the run to safety. It could be used to cut, to kill and even to get him some much-needed food. He could have used it to cut him free of the sail. They would have been gone before the wolves ever found them. This claw could help him survive.

Survive.

Jason knew that would be difficult. Canada had been declared the most difficult place to survive on the planet in the wild. But he also knew he would fight until his last breath. He wasn't exactly a slouch when it came to the wilderness. Jason had always loved camping (just not with wild animals that would tear him apart and kill him) and was an avid Boy Scout. Between what he knew about the wild and that, he could survive until the rescue teams came.

And that had to be soon, right? Right? The world would know that someone was missing, his parents would report it to the police and the police would report it to the army and all of that, and help was going to come finally, right?

Help wasn't coming.

It took Jason three days to figure that out. Three days of watching the skies, listening for planes, and praying that someone, anyone would come for him. Three days of nothing. He had been sitting around in the same area that he was when he hid from the wolves, and he knew for certain that help wasn't coming.

If they were coming for him, they'd have been here long ago. In this part of the country, things tend to die quickly. People die quickly. They wouldn't have dragged their feet when it was a twelve-year-old. No, the only thing they expected to find of him were the parts the animals hadn't liked. And they weren't going to risk more lives to find pieces of a body. They had already decided he had died in this place. And because of that, he would die in this country.

It may not be that day. It may not be the next. But he would die there eventually, and it would probably be soon.

He knew that he should keep up hope for a rescue, but it was hard to be hopeful when you were at the bottom of the food chain. Frustrated, Jason kicked the trunk of a tree. It wasn't fair. He hadn't deserved to land on this godforsaken place. He didn't deserve to be here. He was Jason Smith! He was supposed to be at home in his nice warm bed.

Jason wanted to scream. He wanted to cry. So, he did. He cried for everything he had lost because of those kidnappers and for himself. He picked up a stick and beat it against the nearest tree and let out all the frustration and fear that had been churning inside him ever since he had escaped from the Kidnappers, then sank to the ground as he continued to cry.

All it did was attract the Lizards.

One of the Lizards that he knew, not the scientific name but the local name from a Biology class, was the Red-Golden Lizard. It was one of the very few Lizards that would hunt in packs and was very, very, very savvy with the wild and avoiding larger prey and animals. It was very smart and it knew what to do and what not to do. Alone, the Red-Golden Lizard wasn't anything to fear as it was very small.

But as a pack, it was known to attack, kill and eat larger organisms. And if you were lucky, it was in that order.

The Redgs (a short name for them) were poisonous. There was a neurotoxin in its saliva that made its victim feel befuddled, drowsy, and altogether content.

They didn't even mind when the Redgs began to eat them alive.

The chirping was what first alerted Jason to their presence. The first one hopped into view, looking at him curiously with its reddish-golden skin and deep black eyes. It was the scout. The one that determined whether they would be able to successfully attack their prey.

And in this case, it decided they would attack Jason.

It made an odd chirping noise, and suddenly, there wasn't just one Redg. There was at least a dozen, all surrounding him. Jason quickly shot back to his feet and glanced around. There wasn't anything he could use for a weapon in arms reach.

Sharp pain in his arm drew his attention back to the Lizards. One had leaped onto him and had dug its teeth into his wrist. Quickly, he tore it off, but it was too late. Jason could already feel the ice-cold venom slowly making its way down his arm. He kicked a path in the Redgs and began to run. The sixteen-year-old could hear the strange chirps and hisses as they followed. He ran faster.

Then, he climbed another tree. Jason had a feeling that he'd be getting very familiar with trees soon if he lived that long. He could hear them still hissing and chirping at the base of the tree, but he had the feeling they'd move on soon. They probably had a much shorter attention span than Wolves. For now, he had bigger problems.

The poison.

He wasn't sure if it was fatal or not. The popular consensus had been that it was temporary, only slowing their victims rather than outright killing them. However, no one really knew since the Redgs tended to eat their victims before anyone could find out. And there was no living human specimen of the Lizards as most tended to avoid facing them, or simply killed them all as fast as they could. Besides, there was no way a little Lizard like that would try and eat him, right?

Either way, Jason didn't want it in his body. He yanked off his belt and wrapped it tightly around his upper arm. It would function as a temporary tourniquet. Then, he brought his lips to the wound. They had taught him this in Scouts, but then it had been used for snakebites. This was (just a tad) different. Carefully, Jason began to suck the venom from the bite and immediately spat it out. Then, he repeated the process. He continued until his arm had gone numb from the tourniquet and there was a sour taste in his mouth. He leaned back against the tree and began to fumble with the belt. Finally managing to loosen it, he pulled it off and sighed in exhaustion.

That couldn't happen again. Jason knew that there was every likelihood that he'd be attacked by some other creature, but he couldn't let it happen again due to that reason.

The Redgs were attracted to sick and injured animals, and Jason knew his cries had certainly made him sound like the easy, pre-maimed that the Lizards and other scavengers enjoyed. He had almost been eaten alive because of his outburst back there.

'No more crying' he decided. 'No matter how bad it gets, crying won't help. It'll only make it worse. That is what Grandfather said, remember.'

Jason glanced back down the tree again. The Lizards were gone. He doubted they'd be able to be like the Wolves, actually waiting for him to come back down. Slowly, he began his trek back down the tree. He jumped the remaining distance to the ground and stumbled as he landed. The venom was still making him dizzy, even if it was mostly gone. Steadying himself, he began to move through the woods.

Jason had found a building.

It wasn't a particularly impressive building, but it was a building nonetheless, and it managed to foster hope in Jason that maybe there was a way to call for help.

He should have known better than to hope.

While there were phones, none of them actually worked. There wasn't even any power in the building, nothing electrical in the compound worked. It was supposed to be a Military bunker and when they had abandoned it, they hadn't left any weapons behind; there wasn't anything he could use to defend himself against the Country's other 'residents.'

But that didn't mean he hadn't found anything helpful. The building was a gold mine of information. Apparently, this bunker was supposed to be a bomb testing site and not a normal bomb, but some sort of frag grenade and other C4-like bombs. It wasn't anything Nuclear in nature, but he wouldn't be surprised if there was something that wasn't supposed to be here. He also found the exact coordinates of the building, and the Radio that he had gotten from his captors could be used to get a message to someone out there. What's more, they had left behind supplies. Jason could salvage food, lanterns, and medicine from the building.

He was tempted to stay in the compound, but he knew he couldn't. Within a few minutes of entering the building, he could see signs of Wolves, footsteps, other types of things like claw-marks and their ways of marking their territory. While the building wasn't being used as a den, it was still frequented by the animals. It wasn't a safe place to stay.

Still, Jason couldn't bring himself to leave the first sign of humanity he'd seen since escaping from the Kidnappers. He stayed there that night, curled up in an old desk chair in an attempt to sleep. And he always did wonder if the Nabbers tried to find out where he had gone. It had almost been five days since he had escaped. Surely, they would have tried something.

When Jason was younger, his mother had taken him to a cathedral.

Religion had been another thing his parents had fought about. His father operated an exacting, precise logic. He hadn't believed in something as intangible as God. His mother, however, was driven by wild thoughts and fervent emotion. You don't have to see something to believe in it, she had whispered to him. The best things are the ones taken on faith. Faith had been important to her, Jason remembered. It had driven her to continue to return to church every Sunday, no matter how many fights it caused.

Then, one day, she had taken Jason with her.

Jason hadn't been sure about God. He had been

torn between his parents, unsure about their opposing viewpoints. However, he had come with her that day. And he never forgot that church.

His footsteps had echoed on the floor, the sound bouncing off the walls and multiplying in the air. He had looked up at the glass windows above him and watched as the dust danced through the light and he felt... something. Jason wasn't sure if it was God. If it was faith. But he had felt it weigh on him, the solemn air of something more.

And as Jason walked through the abandoned missile control room, he was reminded of that feeling.

It wasn't the sacred aura that the cathedral had held. It was very, very different. This room held the remains of crossed lines and shattered dreams. It was advanced that really didn't advance at all, just monstrous ideas come to life. Jason felt like something was trying to crawl up his skin and take root, to forever become a part of his mind and soul.

This room was weighed down with a thousand ghosts.

Jason shook his head. The wild was already making him paranoid. While the room was spooky, there was nothing supernatural about it. No ghost was going to come screaming towards him. No monster would leap at him as he turned the corner like in Cheesy B films.

Then, Jason heard the soft sounds of footsteps

behind him, and he re-evaluated his opinion. Normally, he wouldn't have been able to hear anything. The steps were soft, just the barely noticeable pad of bare feet on a solid surface. If it weren't for the impressive resonating acoustics (oh, so like that church so long ago) in the room, Jason would have never been able to hear it. Quickly, he hid behind an overturned table and waited.

It was a wolf. The animal didn't seem to be aware of his presence, not yet at least. It was making leisurely, calm sweeps with its head as it lazily inspected the room. 'What is it doing?' Jason wondered.

Suddenly, the wolf paused and began to sniff the air. Jason's breath caught in his throat. In all likelihood, the thing it was smelling was him. He had to get out of the building. The only problem with that plan was the fact that the wolf was between him and the exit. If he made a run for it, he would be seen and, most likely, killed. The wolf, still sniffing curiously, began to slowly pad its way towards Jason's hiding place. He inched his way backward, only to hit a wall. He couldn't retreat from his position without being seen.

Jason's hand brushed against his pocket. Maybe he could.

While he was exploring the compound, he had discovered smoke grenades. They hadn't seemed particularly useful at the time. They didn't even produce tear gas, just a harmless cloud of vapor. But, they could be used to hide his retreat now. If they worked, that is. He hadn't been able to test them, so there was every chance that they wouldn't work. And if they failed, the wolf would know where he was and he would have nothing to defend himself with.

Jason took in a shaky breath and came to a decision. He'd still be found if he didn't use the grenade. His best chance would be to try it and hope for the best. With unsteady hands, he took the device from his pocket and pulled the pin. Then, he rolled it away from the hiding place and towards the animal. It teetered to a stop right next to the wolf. Jason held his breath as the carnivore bent down to sniff it.

Nothing was happening!

He closed his eyes in defeat. He was dead. Then, an unusual barking sound grabbed his attention. His eyes flew open. The wolf was making a strange, pained choking sound. Smoke was pouring out of the grenade, clouding the air. A smile planted itself on his face as the wolf stumbled backward. It was working. Not wasting time, he sprinted through the cloud and out of the room, skidding into the wall as he turned the corner. He heard the cawing of the wolf as it began to pursue. Jason could see the exit. It was fifty feet away. Forty. Twenty-five. Fifteen. Then, Jason saw it. There was a metal gate that rolled down from the ceiling, like the kind that his dad used in his plumbing supplies store in the mall, at the intersection before the doors. Not breaking stride, Jason tensed his legs and jumped. His hands grabbed the bottom of the grate, and for a horrible moment, he feared it wouldn't move. But then it gave with a screech and came rumbling down towards the ground. Jason tumbled to a stop against the door as it slammed into the ground. Then, an enormous crash brought his eyes shooting towards the partition.

The wolf had slammed into it seconds after it locked into place. Frustrated, it slammed its body into the gate again and again. The metal creaked and bent, but remained locked in place. A small smile touched the corners of Jason's mouth, but vanished the moment the wolf let loose a deep, guttural howling noise.

It was calling for help.

Jason didn't want to be there when help arrived. He pulled himself to his feet and threw open the double doors. Then, he fled into the long grasses, praying that wherever he ended up would be safer than where he left.

Jason found his luck was a mixed bag.

On one hand, he seemed to have found shelter. On the other hand, he may have given himself a concussion in the process.

After fleeing the military compound, he had stumbled into the treeline. He didn't stop, though; he needed to put as much distance between himself and the wolves as possible. He did learn, however, through (quite a painful) experience that he should have slowed down, if only slightly. He had been darting through the branches as quickly as he could when the ground gave out from under him. He tumbled down the newly discovered hill and quite literally clanged to a stop.

Rubbing his head, Jason looked up to see what he slammed into. In front of him was a large water truck that had been trapped in a gorge. Yanking himself to his feet, he began to slowly inspect the vehicle. There was a steel door on the side of the overturned truck. Jason winced as it creaked open. Anything could have heard that. Carefully, he pulled himself through the opening and dropped to the floor within. He glanced around the dreary space. It was dark, damp, and cold. The steel of the walls felt like ice against his skin and there were still puddles of water inside the container. But, there were large metal bolts that could be drawn against the trap door. It could be used to keep animals and insects out.

Jason smiled to himself. This could work. He didn't care what poor sod ended up in such an accident, or how old this water truck was because it did seem like a very old model. This meant two things. There used to be a motorway here and he knew that the ground was strange around the area, he just hadn't noticed it properly. And if there was once a Motorway there years ago, then another one, however unused it was, wouldn't be far. This water truck was a remain along with the Military compound, and it was going to be his hiding place, at least until he got an idea as to where he was and what he was doing. After that, though, this was the only way he was going to be able to escape.

***

The last place Jason wanted to go was back towards the Wolves, but he had no choice. He needed the supplies in the building. Besides, the wolves had probably moved on long ago.

Or at least that was what Jason kept telling himself.

Cautiously, Jason pulled himself out of his new, temporary home and glanced around. There didn't appear to be any animals, insects, Redgs or anyone in sight. He glanced up at the sky. In Scouts, they had learned to tell the time by looking at the sun. Based on Jason's estimation, there was still a good four or five hours of sunlight left. He would need them. Slowly, he set out towards the Military Missile complex. While the trip took quite a bit more time, he avoided cracking his head against the side of a giant metal car again.

He reached the building with no trouble. Carefully, he inched open the doors and glanced inside. There wasn't a wolf in sight; not that meant much. He crept inside and looked around. Immediately, he was thankful he hadn't stuck around earlier. The reinforced steel gate that Jason had used to block the wolf hadn't held up against whatever assistance the creature had called for. All that was left of it was a warped bunch of chains hanging from the ceiling. He began to make his way through the compound, intently listening for any signs of Wolves.

He made his way to the supply room without a confrontation. The Military had kept their facilities well stocked, and they hadn't had any time to clear out before abandoning it. If he carefully rationed it, he'd have enough for years.

If he lived that long, that is.

Jason slowly began to move supplies over to his water truck. He wasn't going to bring everything; that would take too long and take up too much space. Instead, he just brought enough food and lanterns (actually, why did they even have those and how old was this base for them to use bulb lanterns that worked on batteries and not LED flashlights that could last three times as long?) for a few weeks. That way, if something happened that limited his ability to move about the area, he'd be able to hunker down in his truck for at least a couple weeks before coming back. It took a while to move the supplies as he had to make multiple trips, but it was worth it.

Jason tugged a lab coat off its hanger. The water truck was cold, and while the jacket was thin, it would provide at least a little warmth. He swung it on and frowned curiously at the weight inside its pocket. A small, leather journal was resting inside the coat; it must have been forgotten when the Military Base Scientist or doctor had left the base. Jason glanced through it inquisitively. Whoever it belonged to must have just started it as there were only a few pages used, and all of it was in a strange foreign, coded language that the Military had employed. He couldn't understand a word. Shrugging, he slipped it back in his pocket.

Jason glanced around the center. He had already moved all the food he would need and take all the smoke grenades in case he ran into any Wolves. He wouldn't have time for any more trips; he didn't want to be out after dark. He slung the First Aid kit he had found over his shoulder and got ready to leave when something caught his eye. The center had a line of well-stocked vending machines rusting in the corner. While it would be comforting to have a bit of tradi-tional, rot your teeth candy, the power was out. He couldn't exactly shove in a quarter and get a chocolate bar. He glanced around for something to break the

Plexiglass with. While he had been studying Brazilian Jiu-Jitsu since he was a little kid (his security-minded, be-prepared-for-any-eventuality father had insisted on Jason learning self-defense. He hadn't minded as he actually enjoyed the lessons), he didn't trust himself to be able to break the glass with his foot, not without injuring himself. Then, he remembered something. Quickly, he headed back to the other room and rifled through a desk drawer. He snagged a screwdriver from the opening along with a broken bit of a metal bar that had been discarded on the ground and hurried back. There, he rested the head of the screwdriver against the Plexiglass and brought the metal bar down on top of it. A complex pattern of cracks spider-webbed across the surface of the machine. Jason repeated the process and his makeshift tools crashed through the opening. He smirked at the victory and dug out a few of the bars. These would have to be even more strictly rationed than the food.

Carefully, he set back out for his new home, inspecting his surroundings as he went. Jason would have to be on high alert as he traversed the wilderness. With a sinking feeling, he realized he would likely have to be on high alert for the rest of his life unless he found a way to get the hell out of this place.

Jason plopped against the floor of the truck with a sigh. By all accounts, it had been a good day. He had only been attacked by animals once, and he managed to escape without a scratch. He had found supplies and had gained valuable knowledge about how to survive.

'If those are my standards for a good day, something must be seriously wrong with me.' He thought.

Still, he missed his mom and dad, they had been good parents. They never stopped loving Jason, even if they stopped loving each other at times. His eyes burned at the thought of them. He would give anything to see them one more time.

'They probably think I'm dead.' He thought. 'Just like everyone else.'

Jason took a deep breath and forced himself not to cry. He had only promised himself yesterday that he would stop crying; he wasn't about to break that promise. He just wished there was a way to let people know that he wasn't dead yet. Even if it wasn't found for thirty years and he had been killed long before, he wanted them to know that he hadn't died so easily. That he had survived, if only for a little while. With a groan, he turned on his side and tried to sleep.

There was a bulge in his pocket.

Jason remembered the journal he had found earlier and knew that if he didn't manage to escape, someone would have to know where he was and find this place no matter how many years it would take. He knew that he would try his best to get the hell out of whatever part of Canada he was in, but he didn't know how long that would take and it would probably kill him in the end. But he did have a journal. And, one day, it may be found. He sat up, sleep instantly forgotten. This notebook could be a chance, he realized. A chance to say goodbye to his parents, a chance to let them know exactly how long he lasted here. He could let them know that he loved them, even if he wasn't there to say it in person.

Jason yanked the leather-bound book out of his pocket and flipped it open. Scrambling in his pockets for a pen, he pulled that out as well. The low glow of the lantern cast strange shadows on the paper, but Jason didn't mind. Then, he paused. What would he write? What could he possibly say about the situation he was in?

He could hear the noises of the wild outside of his metal walls. The roars of the predators, the howling of the wind, the screeches of pain and fear from the newly prey. This was the closest anyone would ever know about what it was like in prehistoric times, Jason realized, the only way he would understand the life of their ancestors, always fearing for the worst. At least he wasn't actually in those times. He didn't know what he would do if he was actually in such places. Jason guiltily wished that the honor belonged to anyone but him. His resolve strengthened, he lowered the pen to paper and began to write.

I guess I should start with the fact that my name is Jason Smith, I'm sixteen years old, and I'm not dead. Yet.

That night the wind howled, the prey screamed, and the predators roared. But Jason barely noticed.

He was too busy writing. And after he was done writing, he remembered. He had a Radio and the co-ordinates of the buildings.

He thought about it. He knew that he couldn't stay close to the building. Relying on only one thing to get someone out of a problem was a very bad idea, Jason knew that. And that wasn't what he wanted to do. Jason knew that if he was going to be smart about things and be thinking about things, then the only way that he would survive the wild would be if he moved about. If he actually used his brains and moved around the area, and tried to find a way to escape, tried to find a way to live and tried to find a way to get out of the wild. And for that to happen, he would have to leave this place, this water truck, and the compound. But he could at least send a message in.

Remembering everything he could about the various survival tricks he had learned in the Boy Scouts and the shows he had seen on TV, Jason slowly acti-vated the Radio. Upon the first sound of the loud static, he closed it and waited with bated breath, hoping that no one heard it. Luckily, no one had. Nothing was heard and no one had come. So, Jason knew that he would have to muffle the sound. Luckily, he had enough rags to do that, and carefully setting the frequency that was on the piece of paper with the co-ordinates, Jason tried his luck again.

"To any stations, this is Jason Smith. Can anyone hear me?" His reply was cold, hard silence. He knew that this was stupid and that a Military radio station wouldn't work. "I repeat, to any stations, this is Jason Smith, can anyone hear me?"

There was, once again, no reply, and Jason's will dropped. But he remembered. He knew that the military didn't need to acknowledge anything. So, he started talking.

"I am a sixteen-year-old boy that has escaped from his kidnappers by managing to knock them out using a tray. I don't know if this message goes through or not, but I am in the wilderness of Canada around the location with the coordinates--" Jason read out the coordinates. "It belonged to an abandoned military bunker and I am around a twenty-minute walk to the south of the Bunker inside of a water truck. I hope this message travels across. I am a boy from 8, Chester Street, Southern Boulevard, New York, United States of America. Jason. You can contact my parents, Tyler

Smith and Melissa Smith if you wish. I have been missing for approximately twenty-five days. Please, send help. I will be here for five days more and then I will leave. I repeat, please send help."

And then all that was heard inside of the water truck was the cold, hard darkness.

CHAPTER THREE_

JASON PUSHED as close to the end of the branch as he dared. As he predicted, he had become extremely accustomed to trees in his time in the Wilderness. However, it was not due to the reasons he imagined. He still used it as a means to escape carnivores, but recently, he had begun to use them for very different functions.

Like now.

Jason had discovered a valley. It was enclosed by steep sides that funneled into narrow openings at both ends. A long river snaked through the area, and on top of the walls of the valley, there were tall trees that branched over the edge.

That was where Jason was now.

The valley was a thriving ecosystem frequented by herbivores. Bulls marched by the river, bison roamed in herds, and the rare foxes and badgers stampeded through the grass. A part of him wished he could enter the valley itself, even if he knew he would likely get trampled. And that wasn't even the main danger.

The biggest danger was the Wolves.

There were at least three packs of wolves in the fields, Jason had discovered. The first pack nested in an old abandoned maintenance building on the other end of the country. Jason, rightly valuing his life, had never entered the complex. Jason wasn't entirely certain where the second nest was located, but, based on the territory that the pack patrolled, he suspected it was near where he had first encountered the Wolves. That was likely the reason for whatever animals the wolf had killed before coming to get him; he had gotten too close to the den. And the third pack was located on the edges of this valley.

Jason jerked his head towards the sound of the bison howling and huffing and snarling and doing whatever sound they could while they bathed in the water. Immediately, he brought a pair of pilfered binoculars to his eyes and began scanning the field. He had a theory about this behavior and he wanted to see it confirmed.

He smiled in triumph as he saw the bison herd automatically turn their bodies around, swinging their long, defensive horns in a protective arc. The fox clustered closer behind the larger animals, and Jason knew he had been right.

When he had first stumbled on this valley, one of the first things he had noticed was the unusual behaviorisms of the bison and the foxes. They always remained clustered together, regardless of the cross-species differences. Then, he developed a hypothesis.

Jason had learned about it in biology class. In Africa, zebras, with their good sense of smell, and baboons, with their fantastic eyesight, often remained close together because they were more effective against predators as a team. This mutually beneficial relationship had been called inter-species symbiosis. And bison, who possessed incredibly strong defensive horns yet terrible eyesight, would greatly benefit from the weak but clear-sighted foxes. A mutual predator defense, even if one of them said animals was a predator, and the Fox could betray the bison anytime he wanted. But the bison herd was larger than the Fox herd. And even if he had only spent eight days in the water truck, three days longer in the hopes that someone would come for him, he still needed to find out more about these animals.

Now, he just had to locate the predator.

Jason watched as the streaks of greenish-brown darted across the field. Automatically, many of the herds clustered into a defensive form around their children. Jason spotted the aptly named "good mother" of the bison with the babies standing around her, but that wouldn't save them from the wolves. The Gray wolf was a pack hunter and in this deadly cold, things weren't all that easy.

Jason couldn't help but be a little... awestruck at their attack strategies. The killing machines darted in and out of gaps, separating the herd and striking at the weakest links. They quickly dragged away from their kill, snapping at anything that approached. The bison herd thundered and cried, with the one that Jason suspected to be the prey's mother being the loudest, but it was too late. There was nothing they could do to save their children.

They couldn't even leave the valley.

What astonished Jason the most was the fact that the wolves were herding the animals. They had corralled them into space and attacked anything that tried to leave. While the wolves wisely did not hinder the coming and going of some of the predators, like the Grizzly bears that frequented the area, anything small enough to bring down was trapped inside, destined to be struck down at the leisure of the predators.

It was intelligent. It was sophisticated. And it was not what scientists speculated about wolves at all. For them, the wolves were nothing but insane, abandoning, heartless creatures, but it was now that Jason found out, that wasn't the case.

Ironically enough, one of the earliest theories about wolves was closest to reality. They never abandoned their pack mates unless they did the worse of their crimes, or one turned out to be a lone wolf. They would always stay behind for their pack mates and any time one of their pack died, their howls would be deep and loud. And as if mourning with them, the other packs would also howl, loudly at that.

Jason pulled out his journal and hastened to record the behaviors of the animals. Like the trees, his original function for the notebook had changed. At first, it was a way to maybe let his parents know what had happened to him. Now, however, it was part field journal, part how-to-survive-in-this-crazy-country cheat sheet for any future castaways. He did leave a note in the journal for whoever found it, asking that they gave it to his parents if and when they managed to escape.

And that was a big "if."

Jason had tried, of course, to find a way off. He had lugged palm branches up to the roof of the lab and built an 'SOS' message for any passing planes. The problem was, no planes passed over this particular area. It was very rarely used, and no one was actually stupid enough to fly over it for the fear of the distance it had from the nearest airport.

Which meant there were zero results from that attempt at rescue.

Then, Jason had tried to make his way to the borders. He knew that he wasn't all that deep in the country, he just knew it. From using one of the maps inside of the Military bunker and the other store-room on the other side of the entire damned area that he was trapped in, he knew the location of the water truck, and he was only around 100 miles away from the borders, a distance he could travel in one and a half months. But there was one problem. The wolves were very, very smart and didn't allow anyone to leave their 'circle' of influence and their territories.

All of his escape attempts had the exact same results: failure.

Suddenly, the branch he was on shook under him. Jason's eyes shot up, looking for the disturbance, and his breath caught in his throat at the sight that greeted him.

A bear. It was perched on its hind legs to reach the trees, calmly biting off huge mouthfuls of whatever it was eating. Grizzly bears were omnivores, he realized, and they wouldn't only eat meat but could survive off of fruits and berries as well. Jason watched as it fell back to all fours, shaking the ground as it landed due to its immense size, at least compared to him. Then, it bent its maw towards the ground. Curious, Jason leaned over to see what it was doing. A much younger bear, a baby really, was following closely behind its bigger counterpart. The parent was feeding its child, offering it some of the berries still hanging out of its mouth. Jason smiled as it tumbled over itself to get to the food, its little neck unbalancing the still-growing animal. Then, the adult raised back on its hind legs and returned to the tree.

And it looked at Jason.

Slowly, Jason lifted his hand, not breaking its massive gaze. Then, he carefully pressed his hand against the furry animal.

The brachiosaur didn't move away from Jason's caress. It just stared at him with large, intelligent orbs, as if it knew who he was. Bears were supposed to be wild and extremely harsh. But this one was docile. It could sense that he wasn't going to harm and was only observing, so it didn't attack.

Hot puffs of the animal's breath blew on his face, rustling his hair. Shakily, Jason smiled.

Then, the bear pulled back, falling down to the ground, shaking the ground as it landed. It nudged its child with its head and turned around, the two creatures heading off towards the slowly descending sun.

Jason watched them leave. He clenched the fist that had touched the bear. There were no words for what he had just experienced. But he did know one thing...

He didn't hate this Country. He didn't even hate wildlife.

If he had the choice, he'd leave in an instant. He'd go home to his mom and dad and try to move past everything that had happened here. He'd try to forget all the pain and the horror and the suffering he had experienced. But he would never hate the animals. People tended to only see this country as one thing. Some saw it as a fantastic paradise, a world away from their hectic lives in Canada. They only had awestruck images of kindly, parental humans that would allow humans to intrude and meddle with their lives. They saw unintelligent, benevolent creatures that could be poked and prodded without consequence. They saw the illusion the TV had tried to create, and they only saw the human settlements, but not the wilderness. They would never get to see the wilderness. On a level, they knew that the wildlife was dangerous, but they didn't truly understand what that meant. In their minds, humans would always be on the top of the food chain, and no other predator could change that.

Others, like some of the Politicians, only saw this country as a waste of time and money at times, as if it was meant for them to make fun of, but they were wrong. They were all wrong, every single one of them.

This country had more than one side to it. It had predators that stalked and parents that doted and herds that roamed. It was a thousand different things, all mixing together and interacting and alive. This country had animals on it that were complex and intelligent and, yes, dangerous, but undeniably more so if you disrespected them as so many others had.

And Jason didn't hate them for being dangerous. It was just their nature. There was no malevolent intent, just deep-rooted primal instinct that dictated how they lived and survived.

Jason didn't even hate the Wolves. In fact, now he even loved them.

They had killed various innocent animals. Torn them to shreds right in front of Jason. But they hadn't done it out of some kind of sociopathic urge. They killed them because they were either a threat to the nest, an intruder on their territory, or food. It wasn't for murderous sport for some sick and twisted idea of fun.

Only people killed for those reasons.

Jason glanced at the sun and sighed. While there were still hours of sunlight yet, he needed to head back. He always gave himself hours to return to his water truck, so that if there were any complications on the return trip, he'd still get back before nightfall. If there was one thing Jason was absolutely terrified to experience, it was this wild after dark.

Jason assessed the jump in front of him. He had made it before, but that didn't necessarily mean that he could make it again.

The problem was the tree. The tree with the best view of the valley didn't have any branches that were low enough to climb. So, he had climbed the neighboring tree and grabbed onto the closest branch. He had to leap to get to it, but he managed it. Now, however, he had to figure out how to do it a second time. Jason took a deep breath and tensed his legs. Then, before he could change his mind, he jumped. His middle smacked into the tree, knocking the breath out of him. He threw his arms around the tree but was already slipping. At last the second, his hands found purchase. Slowly, he pulled himself up, wincing as he went.

Soon, Jason was back on solid ground. He adjusted his leaf covering and carefully set off through the jungle. He had gotten better at traversing the wild, but that didn't mean it was safe. On the contrary, each time he set out, he encountered new and terrifying obstacles like the mad bears, the coyotes, the Wolverines and some of the feral Bobcats. But he had escaped all of them. Only the wolves gave him some form of a challenge and only the wolves would make him truly look at them as if he was a piece of meat for them.

Slowly, Jason had been mapping the area. Originally, he was planning on staying near the bunker, figuring that was where a rescue party would start if they ever came. But then he realized that after two weeks, he shouldn't stay and find his own ways. That was a week ago. He had left the Bunker with all of his supplies and was running towards the border, the only way that he would live. He knew that if he didn't run and if he didn't get out of the area, then there was a chance that he wouldn't ever be free, that he would still be stuck in that horrendous water truck waiting for a rescue that never came. So, he left.

Somehow avoiding the wolf (oh, who was he kidding? He knew that there was another pack right around the corner), he had traveled around 30 miles away from the bunker, using the maps and the compass that he had found, southwards. Crossing rivers using a blow-up raft that he had found in an unused campsite, literally the only thing that it had, he was moving to the borders and he would have to get there as soon as he could.

He wasn't as familiar with this area, however, and he never would be because he had to continue moving. Jason had to move on ahead and leave behind the area he was in, in the fear of being smelt and being caught, but he didn't want to slow down, not one bit. He knew that if he stayed around, then he would be in deeper trouble. And right now, he was in perhaps the last obstacle before he reached the great flat-land he had seen from that mountain. Sure, climbing up and down the large piece of misplaced rock had been an utter pain, but he needed to do it, and he knew that he could see the light of the borders in the distance. There was a base nearby, and that is where he had to go.

And that is where he would go. Getting down from the mountain and towards the plains in the distance, he knew that he was on the right track. Even if no one had received the message, he knew where he was going and what he had to do. Right now, this was his home and this was where he was going to be. And until he got back to New York, there was nothing else that he could do about it. Nothing. So, he just followed the route, and perhaps his earlier calculations had been wrong because he was sure with the lights that he saw that the base was much closer than anticipated.

What really, really made him nervous was the forest that was in front of the base, the forest that he knew he would have to go through at night. That was the only way he would be able to get to the base, as he had taken a rest in an indentation near the mountain for the entire day, and he wasn't about to waste time slacking around. He had to move and perhaps, in the night, he would be able to move faster.

The only problem was the predators that were on the hunt out here at this time of the night. He didn't want to encounter them, not at all. But he was going to have to risk it because it was the only way he'd escape. And that is how he ended up in that situation in the first place. But looking back at it, he would never regret making that decision, because that was what had saved him.

Jason was in trouble. Very, very big trouble.

It had started with the forest. He stayed too late and, instead of moving, he decided to stay around and search the tracks of some of the other wild animals in the area, and that is how he ended up in such a situation. First, it was the Beavers that he never could find close enough, and how they moved around and possibly made dams.

Then, it was the Skunks. The Skunks were also very, very dangerous and they never moved around in packs as their gases would harm even them if they...... farted against someone.

There also just so happened to have been several dozen of them blocking his path.

Jason had been forced to wait while they moved out of the way. He would have gone around, but one direction took him on a one-way scenic trip directly off the edge of a cliff while the other brought him into known wolf territory. He had seen the tracks and the way they had marked the trees. Instead of those interesting routes, he had decided to wait until the Skunks moved on.

And by the time that began to happen, the night was already at its highest and the most dangerous. Which was why Jason was slinking his way through the darkness, clutching his wolf claw and praying he'd make it back alive.

Contrary to popular belief, the fact that it was a jungle did not mean there were a plethora of trees perfect for climbing. Quite unfortunately, many of the trees were unsuited to escape carnivores. Some did not have branches within reach, others had branches that were too weak to support his weight, while others were too short to avoid the jump of the predators. Jason was hoping he'd be able to find one to spend the night in soon, but he didn't think it was likely that he'd have the chance to even make it up a tree.

Because Jason was being hunted.

He could feel their eyes on him, their hungry gazes boring into his skin. He didn't think it was the wolves; they didn't make any sound while they hunted. These were calling back and forth, closing in surely and steadily.

And Jason had no idea what they were. He clutched his claw tighter and stumbled to a stop. He was surrounded. Days in the wild told him this, he was surrounded.

Even if he couldn't hear them, he'd still be able to tell they were there. Jason could see them. The animals' eyes were glowing in the darkness, like a cat. And slowly, those glowing eyes were inching their way towards him.

Pure, blind, primordial fear clutched Jason's heart. They were the predators. He was the prey. And he had no way of changing that fact. They were Coyotes, dangerous pack hunters that wouldn't even wait to tear him apart, especially since they were hungry, very hungry.

Jason was beginning to distinguish some of the features of the Coyotes in the darkness. They weren't all that big; maybe three or four feet tall. Most of that height was taken up by their legs. On the tip of their feet, they had hard claws that were similar to the wolves. Their jaws were filled with small, sharp teeth and their large, bulbous eyes took up most of their heads.

Jason had an idea. A somewhat stupid, Hail-Mary-play of an idea. The Coyotes were nocturnal hunters;

they had adapted to accommodate this fact by developing massive eyes that are incredibly sensitive to dim light. It helped them to hunt under the dark canopy of the jungle. It also meant they would be incredibly sensitive to bright light. Perhaps sensitive enough to forget all about the easy meal they were in the process of capturing.

Or, at least Jason hoped they were. He had a few flares in his bag; he had gotten the idea from a book he had read long ago. He thought it may provide a distraction for a wolf if he ever ran into one. Now, however, it looked as if it would provide him with a different service. Slowly, Jason began to creep his left hand into his bag. If he moved too quickly, the coyotes would leap; he had to time this right. His palm passed over several of the objects, searching for the right shape.

The eyes got closer. His hand passed over the fluttering pages of his notebook and the small glass vial of wolf pee he kept for emergencies, don't ask where he got it from, but he kept it with him. He grasped the plastic, cylindrical shape of the flare-

Oh, God.

White-hot pain lanced through Jason's side. With a small, strangled shout, Jason raised his right hand, still gripping the wolf claw, and brought it down on the Coyote's head. The makeshift dagger cleaved into its waxy eye, causing it to release its jaws from the clamp-like grip they had on Jason's side with a shrill howl. The animal stumbled away, still shrieking unnaturally.

The sight provided no comfort to Jason. It was too late; the damage was already done.

He fell to the ground with a dull thud. Jason's hand numbly found his side, coming away slick with hot blood. He could feel the neurotoxin or whatever the saliva of the animal contained begin to work its way into his bloodstream. He knew what was going to happen next. The Coyotes would retreat and wait for the poison to wear him down to the point of no resistance. All of Jason's defenses would slowly be battered down by the neurotoxin, causing hallucinations, then seizures, then paralysis, and finally brain death. He didn't even know how Coyotes had such poison in their jaws. Maybe this was a new type, or maybe it was just his damned hallucinations. He just knew that whatever was inside of his blood wasn't supposed to be there and any poison would hurt him, that was certain. And after he was vulnerable due to the bite, infected with whatever was on the jaw of the Coyote, that's when they would come and drag him back to their den, where he would be immediately eaten if he was lucky.

Jason wasn't going down without a fight. He had spent every single second in the wilderness fighting. He hadn't had a moment of peace since he had escaped.

Not. One. Single. Moment.

And he wasn't about to give up now.

When the coyote bit him, the bite felt strange. From the wound, he had been able to feel small, ice-cold tendrils creeping up his arm, leaving his nerves numb in its wake. The bite was different. It shot up his side, blazing hot, leaving every single nerve ending screaming in pain. Fumbling, he yanked the first aid kit out of his bag. There, in the same neat little row, Jason had first found them in, was five small syringes labeled the 'common' anti-venom. He pulled one from the kit and began to feel along his arm. He could feel his adrenaline-fueled pulse pounding against his fingertips. Carefully, he inserted the syringe into the artery and pushed down on the plunger. His face twisted in pain as the new foreign substance entered his body, but he continued to administer the drug. Once he emptied the entirety of the medicament into his bloodstream, he pulled out the syringe and tossed it aside. Then, he yanked off his lab coat. It was too dark to treat the bite mark itself, and he didn't have time to anyway. He did, however, need to staunch the blood flow as much as possible. He pushed the fabric against the wound and bound it tightly to his side with duct tape.

Jason stumbled to his feet, his mind racing. The Coyotes were waiting for the poison to take effect, he knew that. They would wait until he reached the paralysis or shock stage before attacking again. Only, that stage would never come for Jason (or so he hoped). The anti-venom had taken care of that. And, sooner or later, the Coyotes would figure out their bite wasn't working. They would attack again, only, this time, they wouldn't retreat. They would drag him away then and there, taking him back to whatever hell hole they crawled out of. He had a very limited amount of time to escape.

He pulled a small test tube out of his bag. After the various incidents that he'd had with grizzly bears, Jason only kept a limited amount of wolf pee on him, just in case he ran into some of the animals that he didn't want to run into. While he doubted it would completely cover up the scent of blood, it would buy him time. He yanked the cork out of the vial and splashed the pee over his body. Jason didn't think that bears were nocturnal hunters. And if they were, well, he'd take that predator over the other any day. At that thought, an idea struck him. An insane, suicidal idea that would probably get him killed in horrible and creative ways.

The Coyotes were the predators. Jason was the prey. And there was nothing he could do to change that fact.

But the Coyotes weren't the only predators in this area.

He slung his bag back over his shoulder. With his

wolf claw in one hand and a flare in the other, Jason set out into the jungle.

He was an idiot. Hopefully, when this was over, he wouldn't be a dead idiot. The animals had finally figured out something was wrong. The prey wasn't reacting the way it was supposed to...

And now, they were actively hunting Jason.

A Coyote was near Jason. It was sniffing the air, puzzled at why it couldn't smell him. Jason wasn't sure how long that would last, though. The wolf pee wouldn't hold it off forever. He just had to hope it would move on before discovering him. Currently, he was hidden behind a copse of trees, his hands tightly wrapped over his mouth to keep himself from screaming. He cautiously glanced around the wood. The Coyote was still there, making irritating growling sounds into the air. Jason quickly ducked back behind his feeble cover, pressing himself tightly against the trunk as he tried to quiet his shallow breaths. He was hyperaware of everything around him. He could feel the bark digging into his skin and see the trees rustling in the breeze and hear the same sounds of the country that had haunted him every single night. Only, this time, he was out with the noises. He had never truly been as exposed to Canada's nightlife as he was now. Even before he had found his truck, he still had a modicum of safety. He had spent those first few nights high in a tree, strapped in with his belt to keep from falling to the ground below. Never had he been on the forest floor, wounded and vulnerable.

Until now.

Slowly, he peeked around his cover again. The Coyote was gone. He waited several long moments, searching for any sign of the animal, before cautiously leaving his hiding place. He needed to keep moving. Wolf territory was only about ten, fifteen minutes away if he took it at a dead run. He had made harder runs for the Cross-Country team at school.

Of course, back then he wasn't racing something that was trying to eat him. He could make it. He knew he could make it.

Something crashed into him at full speed. Jason hit the ground with a thud, all the air knocked out of him. The flare and claw skittered out of his hands. He struggled to his hands and knees and tried to crawl away, only to be tackled yet again. He and his attacker rolled across the rocky forest floor, coming to a stop a few feet away. Jason looked up at his assailant.

It was the first one he had seen. The same Coyote that had been searching for him before. The same one whose eye he had gouged out.

It had set a trap. And Jason had walked right into it. It crooned in victory, staring down at its prey. Jason was trapped beneath it, flat on his back, pinned down underneath the animal's weight. His hands scrambled uselessly at his sides, searching desperately for something to use as a weapon.

The animal reared back its head, its jaws open, ready to rip out his throat.

Jason's hands closed around a branch. The Coyote's head fell, its teeth descending closer and closer to his exposed flesh...

Only to clamp around the branch Jason had raised at the last moment as protection. Frustrated, the animal yanked its head free. Jason didn't waste a moment. He reared back his makeshift bludgeoning tool and slammed it into the beast's head. It stumbled off of him with a cry, wobbling as it walked. Jason struggled to his knees, raised the bat, and repeated the action. It jerked away, calling for its pack members to help.

Jason really, really didn't want to see what would happen when help arrived. He scrambled over to the site where he was tackled.

'They had to be here.' He needed the flare and claw; he wouldn't be able to get away without them. His hands passed uselessly through the dirt; he couldn't find anything in the darkness.

'Where were they?'

Jason could hear his followers and the predators coming closer and closer, the reinforcements apparently there.

'Where were they? Where were they?'

He wouldn't be able to outrun the Coyotes, Jason knew that. They were too fast, and he was injured. He needs the flare to make them shy away.

'Where were they? Where were they? Where were they?'

The animals were closing in.

'Where were they? Where were they? Where were they? Where were they?'

He saw the flare. It was lying a few feet away next to the wolf claw. He dove forward, grabbing the flare and ripping open the top.

Nothing happened.

Jason's heart stopped.

Then, the torch sparked to life, casting a red glow on the surrounding area as it sizzled in his hand. Jason spun around, thrusting it in the face of the nearest animal. It jerked back with a scream and a howl, its eyes suffering from the sudden glare. Jason grabbed the claw with his free hand and staggered to his feet. He waved the light in a wide arc around him, illuminating the carnivores surrounding him. There were four of them, all of which retreated with a cry. They stumbled off into the jungle, letting loose calls for help.

Jason turned around and ran in the opposite direction. It wasn't over; they wouldn't let their prey slip away so easily. The Coyotes would be back, only, next time, they'd have much more support. He sprinted towards wolf territory, the flare still burning in his hand.

The hunt was on, again. And hopefully, for the final time. But he knew that he wouldn't last long. He was already bitten, injured and extremely tired due to the adrenaline and the pure and utter danger he was feeling inside of his body. He knew that he had to do something about all this before it all came crashing down upon him and he had to work before things went bad, really bad.

So, Jason ran, and he knew the Coyotes followed. They wanted him and, one way or another, they would have him. The only thing was, they would kill him if he was caught, there would be no escape this time around. He had to run, and run, and run and run as fast as he could. And he was going to run as fast as he could, as fast as his legs could carry. He knew that he had to run. And just as he snapped out of the bushes and the forests, he saw the large barriers of the Canadian/American border. And his heart stopped.

He had made it. He had made it to the border, he had made it as CLOSE to his home as he could get, he had made it and there was no other way to explain this. He was home, he was home, he was home.

And right as he was celebrating inside of his head, a Coyote jumped on top of him again, pinning him against the ground. And that is when he realized he was done for. This time, he wouldn't live. He could feel the animal's breath on his skin and he could feel the way it breathed down upon him, its claws ready to tear him out.

Jason planned to lure it into the wolf territory, and it hadn't worked as he had gone in the wrong direction. Perhaps the wolves lived in some other area of the forest? Either way, he had ended up near the border, and now all he had to do was follow it until he reached some patrol and he would be free. But he wasn't free, not now. He was captured, and he was about to die.

'I'm sorry, mum, I couldn't make it.' He said his last prayers. 'I am sorry, Dad, I never became a soccer player. I am sorry, Rax, I was never able to be your best man at your wedding. I am sorry, Selene, I never could ask you out and I am sorry, Grandfather, I wasn't strong enough. Perhaps you can whoop me when I meet you.'

But the pain and the agony and the cold hand of death never came. Instead, what came was the sound of a gun being loaded, and shot right at the Coyote on top of him. Jason's eyes widened as he looked up from where the gunshot had come from, or the gunshots, apparently.

The Coyotes were howling and running, trying to escape, but they were quickly shot down as harshly as they could be. There were no wildlife members to stop them this time, as this was the Canadian National Army. All of the Army members were wearing their green and dark green camo-suits, with their gear on, and all of them were apparently looking at him strangely. Jason was, for a moment, thinking he was dead as if he was in some sick dream. There was no way this was real, right? Like, there was no way that this was actually happening, right? No, this wasn't possible. And that is when all changed when one of them came to him and helped him up. The pain of the bite he had suffered from the cuts he had on him and the survival he had done was bright inside of his head and body. He looked at the man wondrously, a pale-skinned handsome man.

"Are you Jason Smith of New York?" The man asked him in a Canadian accent. All of the other army-members were looking around them, in the dull of the morning light. "The one that made the distress call?"

"Y-yes." Jason nodded, stuttering. "Yes, I am. I am Jason Smith from New York."

"Mr. Smith, I am Colonel James Exton. This is my team." The man introduced himself. "We are sorry if we were late, we just couldn't find a safe way to come to the place, and we had to drive down last night. It took a long time to confirm that you were truly telling the truth. We found the place where the Kidnappers were hiding and we also found the Nabbers, they still hadn't left, afraid that they would be killed by the wildlife. We also found the water truck that you lived in, the military bunker, and followed your path on one of the maps. We saw the flare and it was lucky that we found you."

"W-What do you mean?" Jason was in shock. "Y-you are... you are actually?"

"Yes, sir. We are here to rescue you and bring you home." The man smiled as a jeep suddenly came from behind them. Four of them. "We are your rescue party, and for surviving the wildlife of Canada, we salute you, sir."

And at once, all of them saluted him, and for Jason, it all felt like a dream. Jason nodded and shakily saluted them back, tears already falling from his eyes. Without warning, he hugged the Colonel who didn't look shocked at all. Instead, he only pulled him in, like he was expecting to.

"Thank you." Jason cried hard. He had previously cried for all he had lost and all he had gone through. But this time, he cried because he was safe. Because he was rescued. Because he had survived.

"Please, let our medic look over you first," James said as he let Jason go, and pointed him towards a man waiting for him with his medical bags. "And till then, we will inform everyone that we found you."

But Jason didn't care.

He had survived.

He had lived.

He was strong.

And he was never, ever going to give up.

IN THE END, Jason Smith was taken to Vancouver so he could go through some heavy observations. He had several infections, had mistakenly taken an anti-venom due to hallucinations from the loss of electrolytes, and he had also not had a proper meal for weeks.

Even before Jason had arrived there, his parents were waiting for him, and Jason had never cried as much as he had when in his mother's tearful and tight embrace. He was a sight to see, his long hair, matted due to the dirt, his body littered with scars and his eyes having a haunted look in them.

When Jason returned to America, he was greeted like a hero; greeted like someone that had not only survived the wild but someone that had survived the war. He was greeted by Rax with the biggest bear-hug he could give, by Selene with the largest kiss that he could get and by his other friends and family members with the biggest cheer he could receive. And only when he was home did he realize what had happened.

The kidnappers took him because of his father. They thought they would get large amounts of money out of his father who was a CEO for a tech company. But Jason had survived, he had escaped, he had lived and made it back home. His kidnappers were all US nationals and were facing harsh penalties for the crimes they committed.

And as for Jason? He was never going to forget the wildlife, he was never going to forget the thrill of survival and the fear of death. So, it was no surprise that when he graduated from high school, he chose the career of joining the military and being a marine. Jason was a true survivor.

THE END

www.ingramcontent.com/pod-product-compliance
Lightning Source LLC
Chambersburg PA
CBHW060910190726
48286CB00002B/448